THE DARK REMAINS

William McIlvanney and Ian Rankin

THE DARK REMAINS

Europa
editions

Europa Editions
1 Penn Plaza, Suite 6282
New York, N.Y. 10019
www.europaeditions.com
info@europaeditions.com

Library of Congress Cataloging in Publication Data is available
ISBN 978-1-60945-719-8

McIlvanney, William and Rankin, Ian
The Dark Remains

Book design by Emanuele Ragnisco
www.mekkanografici.com

Cover photo © John Cooper / Stockimo / Alamy Stock Photo

Prepress by Grafica Punto Print – Rome

Printed in the USA

THE DARK REMAINS

OCTOBER 1972

DAY ONE

1

All cities are riddled with crime. It comes with the territory. Gather enough people together in one place and malignancy is guaranteed to manifest in some form or other. It's the nature of the beast. In the awareness of the citizens the condition usually lies dormant. The preoccupations of our daily lives obscure any dramatic sense of threat. It's only intermittently (when, say, an Ibrox disaster occurs or a Bible John hits the front pages) that people may focus on how close to random risk they have been living. They can sometimes experience a renewed awareness that a kind of ubiquitous, threatening strangeness is haunting the edges of apparent normalcy. They realise again how thin the membrane is on which we walk, liable to fall through at any moment into darker places. They may wonder if they are as safe as they thought they were.

Commander Robert Frederick of the Glasgow Crime Squad was thinking of these things. He was aware of a potential risk that his city might be about to have that comfortable sense of security disturbed. A man called Bobby Carter had disappeared. His family had that afternoon informed the police that he hadn't been home for the past two days. This in itself, as far as Frederick and his squad were concerned, wasn't exactly a cause for deep mourning. Bobby Carter was a career criminal. Or rather, a venally clever lawyer who didn't so much rub shoulders with criminals as steep in the same polluted bathwater as them. Well educated and from a decent family, Carter had chosen to spend his professional life protecting and guiding the scum of Frederick's particular patch of earth. His job was to move dirty money around, putting it out of reach of the taxman. Cash was made clean by buying out law-abiding and fruitful businesses, and it was Carter's remit to ensure that the contract always favoured buyer rather than seller.

As he sat staring across his obsessively tidy desk, what worried the Commander was the vacuum Carter's disappearance might create in the Glasgow criminal fraternity and the violent forces that might rush in to fill it. Carter was known to be Cam Colvin's right-hand man, one of the few he trusted. Colvin's was a name to instil fear, a reputation stretching back to teenage years when he had strode into a surgery demanding to see the doctor. Asked what the problem was, he had said nothing, instead turning round to show the receptionist the blade jutting out from between his shoulders. Cam Colvin decidedly wasn't a man to be toyed with or crossed, which meant that the implications of Carter's vanishing act might reverberate far beyond gangland and affect the greater, wholly innocent population.

The Commander's thoughts were interrupted by a knock at the door. Without waiting to be asked, Detective Sergeant Bob Lilley entered, closing the door after him.

"What's the thinking?" the Commander enquired.

Lilley took a deep breath. "One view is, here's hoping he's been abducted by aliens and taken to another galaxy."

"Who said that?"

"The new boy."

"Laidlaw?" The Commander watched Lilley nod. "Actually, I wanted to talk to you about him."

"Jack Laidlaw is not an unknown quantity, sir. His reputation has always preceded him, which I'm guessing is why we've been landed with him. Who has he rubbed up the wrong way this month?"

"Who's left?" Frederick shifted in his chair. "But the same message keeps coming through—he's good at the job, seems to have a sixth sense for what's happening on the streets."

"I sense a 'but' in the offing."

"Only insofar as he needs careful handling if we're to get the best out of him."

"I'm not much of a one for babysitting, sir."

"It's just for a week or two, until he gets to know our ways."

Lilley considered for a moment before nodding his agreement. Frederick allowed himself to relax a little.

"I'll see you at Ben Finlay's drinks tonight?"

"Don't you worry, sir—I want to make sure the bugger really is retiring this time."

"See to it that Laidlaw's there, too. Let the team get the measure of him."

"Finlay's already invited him. Seems they're old friends. That's a black mark against our new recruit right there." Lilley paused. "I'm assuming there's no news of Bobby Carter then?"

"I should be asking *you* that."

"We've been to talk to the family. Checked his office in town. They waited a couple of days before phoning us because it's not unknown for him to take a deep dive occasionally."

"Meaning?"

"A night at the casino followed by a day sleeping it off wherever he ends up."

"But not on this occasion?"

"No establishment on our radar claims to have had his business."

"Spoken to his associates yet?"

"I'm still hopeful that won't be necessary, because once we've had words with Cam Colvin, we'll have to do the same with the opposing teams."

"Meaning John Rhodes and Matt Mason." The Commander nodded slowly. "Softly softly, Bob, just like the TV show."

"But with a bit more realism, eh, sir?" Lilley turned to leave.

"Eyes on Jack Laidlaw, Bob. I want him inside the tent, as Lyndon Johnson says—if you take my meaning."

Lilley nodded again and was gone, leaving his boss to recommence his staring contest with the closed door. Abducted by aliens was certainly a better outcome than some he could think of.

2

Conn Feeney was counting the house. It didn't take long. The Parlour used to be a busy place. When the shipyards had been at their most productive, they could be six deep at the bar on pay night. At the time he shook hands on buying the pub, after his win on the football pools, it had seemed like a good investment. It was certainly better than working in the yards. He had never felt secure there. He remembered taking Tara to the pictures once when she'd been eight or thereabouts. They were walking hand in hand when a man called across the street to him, "Aye, Willie!"

"Aye, Tam," he'd called back. "Nice night."

As they walked on, Tara had asked why the man had called him by the wrong name.

"He's got me mixed up with someone else," he'd explained.

He hadn't wanted to add another fault line to her innocence. He was known as Willie McLean in the yard because that was the name he'd given them. Back in the day, adding Connell Feeney to an application form would have been like including a Hail Mary and a sprinkling of holy water. Catholics were not yet welcome in the Protestant fiefdom of the Clydeside yards.

"Fiefdom" was a good word. The long self-education to which he had submitted hadn't been wasted. He often thought to himself, you're too good for here, before remembering he owned the place. The Parlour was *his* fiefdom. Schooldays had been little more than a stretched-out assumption that he and his kind were destined for manual labour. He'd eventually proved his teachers wrong, to a degree.

Then again, where was the evidence? These days you could prefix "Funeral" to the pub's name and it wouldn't seem out of place. He cast a practised eye over his clientele, all five of them. Auld Rab was at his usual table, getting solemnly and quietly plastered. Presumably it numbed whatever was troubling him, psychic or physical. His wife was dead, his children had moved away and never called or wrote. He seemed to be biding his time until they came to collect the remains.

Susie and Marion were having one of their regular "girls' nights." All dressed up and nowhere to go except memories and anecdotes recalled from their younger years. They sometimes dug blurry photographs from their shoulder bags, holding them up for Conn to admire. Short skirts, thickening legs, eyes excited by thoughts of the future. They giggled a lot even now and drank Cinzano and lemonade with a slice, meaning Conn had to stop in at the nearby greengrocer's once a week for a solitary lemon.

The other two drinkers he didn't know. A young man and a young woman. He'd already decided he didn't like the look of the man. He sat with one arm draped over the back of his companion's chair, while the other lay on the table in front of her. It was as if he were constructing a wall around her. Any minute now he'd be adding barbed wire and a No Trespassing sign. He spoke directly at her face, keeping his voice low but insistent. She couldn't be much more than eighteen and he was no older than twenty. She looked uncertain, as if trying to gauge the safest route around the avalanche tumbling from his mouth.

Conn recognised a Glasgow seduction when he saw one. He was glad both his daughters were safely married. When the couple rose suddenly and the girl stooped to pick up her umbrella, he couldn't resist lobbing a remark their way, like a coin towards a wishing well.

"Safe home, the pair of you. It's a dirty night."

The young man leered at him in what seemed both hope and expectation. When the door closed on them and Conn crossed the floor to collect their glasses, he noted that the girl had barely touched her drink. That might be a good sign. She was keeping her wits about her. By the time he was back behind the bar and running the tap in the sink, he realised that Rab had completed the long day's journey from his table.

"Should have given me a shout," Conn told him. "I'd have brought it over."

"Doctor says I've to get some exercise. I told him I'll get plenty when they shut the surgery. It's moving a mile and a bit away. Half a dozen white coats and you won't get a say in which one sees you. Tell me, is that meant to be progress?"

"You'll need a pair of gym shoes, Rab."

"Ever tried polishing a pair of those?"

"I can't say I have."

"That's why I won't be wearing them. My father said never to trust a man who didn't own good leather shoes."

Conn nodded and decided not to remark that tonight, as usual, Rab was wearing tartan carpet slippers whose rubber soles were starting to perish. Instead, he hit the whisky optic twice and set the refilled glass on the counter as Rab fumbled in his pocket for the necessary coins.

"This one's on the house—just don't tell the management."

"You're some man, Conn."

"Maybe you could tell my wife that."

"I would, but she never comes in."

"She finds the place a bit too highfalutin." Conn pretended to examine his surroundings. "The crushed velvet and the candelabras."

He seemed to have lost Rab, who was already doing a slow turn, ready for the thousand-yard walk back to his table. The sound of the door to the outside world being yanked open alerted Conn to trouble. But it wasn't skinheads or one of the other local tribes. Cold air entered along with a gust of rain. The young couple stood on the threshold, unsure what to do next. They seemed hardly to recognise the premises they'd just left. Eventually they shuffled inside, the door clattering shut behind them. The umbrella was half open. Conn wasn't sure at first if those were raindrops or tears on the woman's chalk-white face. Her partner's cocksure patter had left the stage. When he found his voice, it was louder than necessary.

"We found a body," he announced.

"Where?" demanded Conn.

"The back lane."

"A tramp?" Susie piped up.

"Big guy, well dressed. That's as much as we saw."

Conn was weighing things up. The police would need to be informed, but was there anything he should do first? Would they want to check his accounts or open the safe? He doubted it. Should he alert John Rhodes? But then would that look like he thought there might be a connection?

"You sure he's dead?" he asked, playing for time.

"Unless he just likes lying spread-eagled in a handy puddle."

"Go take a look, Conn," Auld Rab suggested.

It was one way to defer the inevitable, Conn supposed. He reached to a hook for his jacket and it was as if he'd pulled off a conjuring trick. All eyes were on him, the sleepy room suddenly animated.

"Is it all right if we grab a drink?" the young man was asking as Conn made to pass him.

"Wait till I get back," Conn said in warning. He opened the door and stepped out into the dark.

The rain was easing, leaving pools of water for him to navigate. The lane was just that. It led behind the bar to where bins and empty crates were stored. The bins were galvanised, their lids long gone, taken by kids to use as shields or paired to make unholy cymbals. Between them, he could see the body. He tried to think when he'd last been out here. Not for a couple of days. The man wore a suit. He lay on his front, his red tie resembling a ribbon of blood. His head was angled so that his face was visible, the thinning black hair sticking to it.

"Bobby bloody Carter," Conn muttered. "Cheers for that, Bobby. Aye, that's just what I need . . ."

He retreated to the bar. It looked as though no one had moved a muscle in his absence. He kept his jacket on while he poured himself a vodka, downing it neat and in a single gulp.

"Well?" the young man asked him.

"What are you having?" Conn Feeney enquired.

3

The Top Spot, a bar on Hope Street, was the usual watering hole of choice. It was crowded when Bob Lilley arrived. Even so, Jack Laidlaw seemed a man apart, easy to spot, almost as if he had a radioactive glow. Ben Finlay was seated at a table, surrounded by drinks he hadn't got round to yet and discarded wrapping paper. One retirement gift, a copy of *Playboy*, was being passed around, its centrefold unfurled. The female faces scattered around the room wore tight smiles, knowing they were expected to play along. They were ancillary staff mostly—the infamous typing pool—plus one or two constables, hardly recognisable in civilian clothes and freshly retouched make-up.

Lilley weaved his way through the crush until he reached the bar, where Laidlaw was alternating sips of whisky and puffs on a cigarette. He was a handsome enough man, broad-shouldered and square-jawed, but he managed not to look too happy with his lot, as if, in his late thirties, life had already subjected him to a harsh interrogation. He brought baggage with him—Lilley knew at least a few of the stories—but judgement could wait.

"Tried to catch you at the station. I'm DS Lilley. Bob to you." He held out a hand, which Laidlaw shook, raising one eyebrow afterwards.

"A fellow member of the non-Masonic fraternity," he commented.

"Failed the audition when I burst out laughing. What can I get you?"

"Antiquary."

The barman had appeared in front of them, a sheen of sweat on his forehead. "First drink's already paid for, Bob," he said.

"Two Antiquaries then."

"We've John Rhodes's largesse to thank apparently," Laidlaw explained.

"So we're taking drinks from gangsters now?"

"Why break the habit of a lifetime? Besides, it's nice to be nice—John understands that."

"You know the guy?"

"We've had our moments."

"How about Cam Colvin?"

"Not so much. He's a thug who surrounds himself with others who remind him of himself."

"And John Rhodes doesn't?"

"John likes men who are scarred on the inside as much as the outside, but he's not like that himself." Laidlaw finished his first drink as its replacement arrived. He looked around the bar. "Have you noticed how police never just visit pubs? It's more like temporary ownership."

"Looks to me like the student union at Stirling Uni gearing up for the Queen's visit." Lilley gestured towards Finlay's table. "Did I miss the speeches?"

"There was just the one—Commander Frederick. He knew the lines by heart. 'Conscientious,' 'much valued,' 'irreplaceable.'"

Lilley gave a snort. "His replacement's already in post."

"Do I take it you aren't a fan?"

"Ben's a nice enough bloke, team player and all that. But he couldn't detect shit in a cowshed."

"I've always liked him. He gave me some good advice once."

"Oh aye?"

"When he was working a case, he said, he often stopped the night at a hotel in town. Saved him the commute and meant he kept his head in the game."

"Well, he might have a point there," Lilley conceded. "Like a surgeon binning the surgical gloves before going home. You don't want the job going with you and contaminating the evening meal."

"I'd need a new head every day, Bob, and not even the Barras is selling them." Laidlaw was taking a fresh cigarette from the pack. He offered one to Lilley, who shook his head. A hand landed heavily on Lilley's back. He swivelled to face a grinning Ernie Milligan.

"All right, Bob?" Milligan said.

"This is DI Milligan," Lilley told Laidlaw.

"Jack already knows me," Milligan interrupted. He made show of studying Laidlaw's apparel. "Get yourself to Rowan's, man, tell them I sent you. You look whatever the opposite is of professional." Then, to the barman: "Two lager, two heavy."

Milligan's face was flushed and his tie askew. His hair was already turning grey and he wore it longer than the Commander liked, his defence being that it helped him blend in, much as a barn door would blend in at a festival of garden rakes. Lilley had watched the change come over Laidlaw, his entire edifice tensing in Milligan's presence, like a trap that's had its camouflage brushed aside.

"We were DCs together once upon a time," Milligan continued, seemingly unaware of his proximity to six-feet-plus of unalloyed enmity. "One of us has kept climbing the ladder, the other's still at the bottom, petrified of heights." The tray of pints had arrived, Milligan gripping it firmly, offering a wink in Laidlaw's direction before ploughing into the crowd again.

"See, I don't mind coppers like Ben Finlay," Laidlaw said quietly. "He might not be hugely gifted, but he knows right from wrong."

"You're saying Ernie Milligan doesn't?"

"I'm saying he'd be just as happy in a uniform with a swastika on the sleeve. As long as he was left alone to do the job the way he reckoned it needed to be done, he wouldn't complain or even stop to think."

"Why do I get the feeling you've told him as much to his face?"

"Sometimes you have to judge a book by its cover. There's nothing in Milligan's pages that you couldn't glean from a moment's look at him." Laidlaw finished his whisky.

"Speaking of books, I happened to be passing your desk. Not quite the usual *Criminal Law* and *Road Traffic Law* . . ."

Laidlaw almost smiled. "Unamuno, Kierkegaard and Camus."

"Reminding us you studied at university?"

"I left after a year, not sure that's anything to shout about."

"What are they for, then?"

"We know where a crime ends," Laidlaw obliged. "It ends with a body maybe, a court case, someone going to jail. But where does it begin? That's a much thornier question. If we could work back to those origins, maybe we could stop crimes from happening in the first place."

"Crime prevention already exists."

Laidlaw shook his head. "It's not cops like you and me we need so much as sociologists and philosophers. Hence those books."

"I'd like to see Socrates patrolling the Gallowgate on an Old Firm night."

"Me too. I genuinely would."

The phone had been ringing behind the bar for a couple of minutes, the barman finally finding a moment's breather that allowed him to answer, hand pressed to his free ear to shut out the din. He scanned the room, said something into the receiver, and left the handset dangling while he went in search of someone, returning a moment later with the Commander. Whatever information Robert Frederick received seemed to sober him up. The nearest bodies belonged to Lilley and Laidlaw, and he fixed them with a look. Having replaced the receiver, he faced them across the bar, as if about to proffer an unexpectedly large drinks bill.

"You've not long arrived, Bob?" he checked.

"Sorry I missed your speech, sir. Jack filled me in on the highlights."

Frederick ignored this. "I need the pair of you to scoot to a pub called the Parlour. Body found in the alley behind it. Word is it could be Bobby Carter."

"That's in the Calton," Laidlaw stated. "John Rhodes territory."

"Which is why we need to tread carefully. It'll be a while before this lot will be any help, but we'll be there when we can."

"Message received," Lilley said.

"And understood?" Frederick's eyes were on Laidlaw.

"Absolutely," Laidlaw replied, his gaze on the ashtray as he stubbed out his cigarette.

4

One look at the corpse was enough for Lilley and Laidlaw. They retreated to the Parlour, leaving the crime-scene crew to it. An ambulance and two patrol cars were parked kerbside, lights flashing. Like smoke signals, they had brought the local tribe from its tepees. The Parlour was doing brisk business. One table was being granted breathing space, though. At it sat a young couple who weren't going to remain a couple for much longer, judging by their body language. While Lilley headed to the bar, Laidlaw sat down opposite them.

"I'm DC Laidlaw," he told them. "You're the ones who found the body?"

Nods from both, their eyes fixed on the array of untouched drinks in front of them. Everyone in the bar, it seemed, wanted to say they'd stood them a round. This was their fifteen minutes of fame, but the clock was ticking.

"A car will take you to the station so we can get a statement. You didn't see anyone?"

"Nobody still able to draw breath," the young man said, affecting a scintilla of what Laidlaw suspected would be his usual swagger. He wore a checked jacket and open-necked denim shirt. There were home-made tattoos on the backs of his hands, probably dating to his schooldays.

"What's your name, son?" Laidlaw didn't bother taking out his notebook. They'd be telling the same story in an interview room soon enough. All he was doing here was making an assessment for his own benefit.

"Davie Anderson."

"And what do you do, Davie?"

"Motor mechanic."

"Steady work, I would think. How about you, love?"

"I'm Moira."

"And could Moira's mum and dad afford a surname?"

"Macrae."

"Moira's a waitress at the Albany Hotel," Anderson added.

"Posh place. That where you met?"

"It's not Rolls-Royces I fix. We met at the disco."

"This your first proper date?"

"Second."

Laidlaw pretended to examine their surroundings. "You certainly know how to treat a lady, Davie."

"We had a Chinese."

"And then in here for a nightcap, rather than Joanna's or the Muscular Arms." Laidlaw nodded his understanding. "After which I'm assuming the back lane was your idea? Pair of you still living at home, no chance of any action indoors. Not a great night for it weather-wise, but needs must . . ."

"He said it was a shortcut." Moira Macrae bristled, folding her arms, creating a barricade that was not going to be breached.

"All I had in mind was a snog," said Anderson.

"The kind of snog that requires a dark alley rather than a bus stop?"

The young man glared at Laidlaw. "We found a dead body, in case you're interested."

"Everything interests me, son. It's what you might call a curse. You didn't recognise the victim?"

"Is that what he is?" Moira Macrae was staring at him. "We weren't sure."

"He was stabbed, as far as we can tell. Autopsy tomorrow will tell us more, hopefully. We think his name's Bobby Carter. Does that mean anything to either of you?"

Laidlaw watched them shake their heads. A drinker had appeared at his shoulder, placing two fresh glasses on the table.

"Just to help with the shock."

Laidlaw turned towards the man. "They're liable to go into cardiac arrest if they drink half what's already here." The look he gave was as effective as wasp-killer, the man backing away in mazy fashion towards the safety of the swarm. Two uniforms were collecting contact details from various tables. Laidlaw crooked a finger towards one of them.

"We need our two witnesses here taken to the station. We also need them relatively sober, so grab a tray and dump this lot." He nodded towards the array of drinks.

"Hell of a waste."

"A thought that often passes through my head when I look at a uniform." Laidlaw was up on his feet. Four short strides took him to the bar, where Bob Lilley had a keen audience for his conversation with the barman.

"We could do with clearing this place," Laidlaw commented.

"You're joking, aren't you?" the barman said. "This is the busiest I've been in months."

"Maybe you can arrange for a murder to become a regular thing. You could announce it on a board outside. If you need any help, I'm sure John Rhodes would oblige. This is his patch, after all, which means you'll be handing a percentage of your takings to him. I'd imagine two sets of books come in handy for that."

An impressive range of emotions had passed over the man's face as Laidlaw spoke.

"Don't know who you're talking about," he said.

"That's the best you can do? What's your name anyway?"

"This is Conn Feeney," Lilley broke in. "He owns the place."

"Nobody 'owns' anything in the Calton," Laidlaw corrected

him. "They're all in hock to John Rhodes." He turned his attention back to Feeney. "You saw the body?" Feeney nodded. "Recognised it?" Another nod. "Mind if I ask how?"

"Plenty people know Bobby Carter."

"Did he ever drink in here?"

"I wouldn't think so."

"No, because he was Cam Colvin's man, and Cam Colvin is going to wonder how come his good friend and associate ended up skewered like a kebab behind one of John Rhodes's pubs."

"This is *my* pub, bought and paid for." Feeney's hackles were rising. Laidlaw took his time lighting a cigarette.

"And still being paid for, I'm willing to bet." The smoke billowed from his nose. He noticed that Lilley's notebook was sitting on top of the bar, a pen resting against a blank page. "Got enough to be going on with?" Laidlaw asked him.

"Hard to tell," Lilley answered.

"Well, don't let me stop you. I'll be waiting in the car."

The car, however, was not where Lilley found him five minutes later. Lilley's Triumph Toledo sat across the street, unoccupied. Laidlaw was patrolling the pavement, scanning darkened tenement windows.

"What was he doing here, Bob?" he asked when Lilley caught up with him. "It's both enemy territory and a nightlife black hole. You've got the Parlour, and a Chinese restaurant at the far corner by the main road. One chip shop. Flats for those who wish they could afford elsewhere. A couple of builders' yards. Bits of wasteland waiting for a developer with more money than sense."

"Is this you playing Socrates?"

Laidlaw wasn't listening. Lilley had become little more than a wall he could bounce words off. "Meeting someone in the pub? Thinking better of it—too small, too much curiosity—so opting for the lane? Meaning it was someone he knew and trusted?" He flicked the remains of his cigarette onto the rutted tarmac.

"Questions for tomorrow," Lilley suggested, paying sudden and conspicuous attention to his wristwatch. "Need a lift home?"

"I'll be fine."

"Whereabouts do you live anyway?"

"Simshill."

"Married?"

"Three kids."

Lilley seemed to be waiting for Laidlaw to ask about his own marital arrangements, but instead Laidlaw turned and began to walk towards the main road, lost in thought once more. Halfway along, he stopped and studied the exterior of the bar again. He was still there when Lilley drove past.

"Odd bugger," Lilley said under his breath. He wondered if anyone would still be at the retirement do . . .

DAY TWO

5

Lilley was locking the Toledo next morning when he saw Laidlaw walking towards Central Division. It was a red-brick building, occupying the corner of St. Andrew's Street and Turnbull Street. Laidlaw was eyeing the place warily, as if suspecting booby traps. He tensed upon noticing a figure crossing the street towards him, relaxing as he recognised his colleague.

"You don't drive?" Lilley asked him.

"I prefer buses. They open your eyes to the city around you. Though I sometimes take a Glasgow ambulance when funds allow or the need arises."

Lilley knew he meant taxis. He looked Laidlaw up and down: same suit, shirt and tie as the previous day. "You didn't go home last night," he stated.

"Little wonder they made you a sergeant."

"So where did you sleep?"

"The Burleigh. It's the hotel Ben Finlay introduced me to. And to answer your next question, it's just that sometimes home feels too far away."

"Your wife doesn't mind?"

"Her name's Ena, by the way."

"And mine's Margaret. We've two daughters, both adult enough to have left home."

Laidlaw almost smiled. "It's been preying on your mind that I didn't ask." They began climbing the steps to the station together. "So what's on today's message list?"

"We'll soon find out. And you're wrong about that 'preying on your mind' thing."

"I'm not, though, am I?" Laidlaw yanked open the door and preceded Bob Lilley inside.

Glasgow's mortuary, adjacent to the High Court and across from the expanse of Glasgow Green, was a study in anonymity, single-storeyed unlike its grandiose neighbour and visited only by brisk professionals and the grieving bereaved. The deceased's wife had been brought there in the wee small hours to identify the body. As Laidlaw and Lilley reached the viewing room, they realised the post-mortem examination was already over. The body was being sewn together by an assistant, who kept his nose pressed close to the flesh as he worked. Laidlaw hoped it was a case of myopia rather than ghoulish pleasure. Heading back into the corridor, they were in time to catch the pathologist. He still wore his scrubs, over which a bloodied apron stretched from mid-chest to his knees. The green wellingtons on his feet reached to just past his ankles. He was drying his hands as the two detectives approached.

"We were told ten sharp," Laidlaw said.

"You were misinformed."

"Our boss isn't going to like that," Lilley added.

"Pleasing your boss isn't my number-one priority, DS Lilley. Now do you want the glad tidings or not?" Neither man answered, no answer being necessary. "Five stab wounds, all from the same knife. Probably an inch-wide blade. Deepest incision is four inches. It went up from under the ribcage, piercing the heart. Almost certainly the fatal blow. Where it came in the pecking order, I can't say. No signs that he defended himself—no nicks on his hands, for example. It wasn't a machete, a craft knife or a razor."

"Not a teenage gang then," Laidlaw stated.

"Speculation is your game; facts are mine."

"How long has he been dead?"

"Two or three days. His possessions are on their way to the lab, along with his clothes and shoes."

"Money in his pockets?"

"Just shy of sixty pounds."

"Probably rules out a mugging, then," Lilley commented.

"A good make of watch, too—Longines. The shirt and jacket were Aquascutum. I believe the family home is in Bearsden."

"Even people with money end up dead sometimes."

"Especially ones with friends like Cam Colvin." The pathologist seemed pleased with the effect his words had. "He was with the widow for the identification. Handled her with great gentleness, I must say."

"Did he speak to you?" Laidlaw enquired.

"I kept a respectful distance."

"Respectful as in fearful? Who was here from our side?"

"Our mutual friend." This time the look was for Laidlaw only.

"Milligan?" he guessed.

"DI Milligan tells me he's been put in charge of the inquiry. That must fill you with as much confidence as it does me, DC Laidlaw."

"Did Milligan and Colvin talk?"

"A few words as they were leaving."

"How did the wife seem?"

"Completely devastated. It's why we have soundproofing."

The three men fell silent as the trolley bearing Bobby Carter's corpse was wheeled out on its way to one of the fridge drawers. A sheet had been draped over the whole. Laidlaw had a mind to ask the attendant to stop so he could take a look at the dead man's face, but he didn't.

There would be photographs back at the station. Lots of photographs.

Lilley thanked the pathologist and turned to go. Laidlaw hung back, however.

"Did Milligan know what time the autopsy was due to start?"

The pathologist gave a nod. "Maybe it just slipped his mind," he said.

"Aye, or else he decided to have a bit of fun with me and DS Lilley."

"When something's 'a bit of fun,' people are generally amused."

"I'm laughing on the inside," Laidlaw said as he started to follow Bob Lilley out of the building.

6

So one funeral's already in the planning and it's put me in the mood for another. Only thing is, this one will be a bit more private—the foundations of a motorway flyover would be ideal. You get what I'm saying?"

Cam Colvin looked at each face in turn across the polished oval table. He'd summoned his men to the function suite of the Coronach Hotel. The manager, Dan Tomlinson, had seen them settled with tea, biscuits and a jug of water. After he'd left, Colvin's look intimated to the others that, even supposing they'd just stumbled from the baking heat of a parched desert, they weren't to touch anything. He wanted them focused on his words and his demeanour.

Colvin was not the biggest of men, yet he filled a room without effort. His face was a locked door, with a peephole through which he studied and learned. He had draped his black three-quarter-length Crombie coat over the back of his chair and run a hand through his hair to push it back into place. The cut was slightly long, as though Teddy boys had never gone out of fashion. Ever since his early teens his reputation had been growing. He'd run with a gang and fought with unusual ferocity, never backing down no matter the threat level. But he was savvy, too, and cautious in matters of business. The men gathered here were the few he genuinely trusted. To others it might have resembled a committee of gargoyles, but in Colvin's line of work you didn't want staff whose looks put people at ease.

"I'm judge and jury on this one," he went on, "and sentence

has already been pronounced." He ran a finger down the front of his dark tie, as if to ensure nothing was out of place. "But he's alive when he gets to me, understood? It's my job to do the necessary dismantling, and that process will maybe take a while." His eyes scanned the group again. They were still paying attention. There was an empty chair to Colvin's right. Past that sat Panda Paterson, Mickey Ballater, Dod Menzies and Spanner Thomson. Panda's love of food would normally have had him on his third or fourth biscuit by now, but he knew to behave himself, today of all days.

"This is a message to us. It's telling us something. Somebody out there thinks we'll leave it alone? No chance. I want you to start asking around, and don't feel you need to be subtle about it. It's fast answers I'm after, not diplomacy. See this chair here?" He patted it. "This is where Bobby should be sitting, and it needs to be filled. Hopefully by whichever one of you brings me the news first." He paused, letting the invitation percolate. "So give me some ideas—where would you start looking?"

"Pub's an obvious one," Panda Paterson said, his voice like slurry. "It's on John Rhodes's turf, though."

"No 'though' about it," Colvin snapped. "Territory's a thing of the past until this gets solved."

"What about Jenni?" Dod Menzies offered.

"Jenni's difficult," Colvin said, shifting in his seat.

"The wife doesn't know?"

"Bobby was always clever that way. I'd rather Monica didn't find out. She's got enough on her plate, before you factor in the kids. Besides, stabbed behind a pub—does that sound like a crime of passion to you? No, this was business."

"Which brings us back to John Rhodes," Spanner Thomson piped up. He had a reedy voice, one that sometimes caused strangers to chuckle or tease him, which they did only until the heavy spanner—his implement of choice—was drawn from his inside pocket.

Colvin pressed his hands together. "I'll maybe be needing a word with John. But let's hold off and see if he comes to us first. Other routes we should be travelling?"

"Bobby had no shortage of enemies, boss," Mickey Ballater offered. "You know that. He was a good enough fixer but lousy at keeping his head down. Number of times I've had complaints from clubs and restaurants he walked out of without paying. Anybody resisted, he reminded them who he worked for."

There were nods around the table.

"I don't suppose you've ever done that, Mickey? Or you, Dod? We're all family here, right? Don't go speaking ill of the dead." Colvin paused. "Okay, the man had a bit of history and maybe you need to dig into that. What worries me, though, is how blatant the killing was. Either someone's putting Rhodes in the frame—someone like Matt Mason—or else Rhodes himself thinks he's bulletproof. That's why I see it as a message we need to decode. Not easy for people whose only paper qualifications are for truancy, but that doesn't mean you're not going to work flat out. I want you busting your gonads on this. Okay?"

Once the nods around the table had satisfied him, he got to his feet and produced a tray from a cupboard. It held a bottle of whisky and six glasses. He poured the measures with due ceremony and handed them round, leaving one in front of the empty chair.

"Bobby was a valued member of our team, one who kept us a bargepole's distance from any whiff of fraud or tax evasion. So here's to absent friends." He raised his glass in a toast.

They drank in silence. Paterson swallowed and wiped his mouth on his shirt cuff.

"Okay if I have a biscuit now, boss?" he asked.

"Your dentist must love you almost as much as your doctor," Colvin muttered, rising to his feet. "I'm away for a pish. Don't let me detain youse."

After Colvin had left, Paterson ran a tongue around his mouth. "At least I've got all my own teeth, mostly," he commented, reaching for the plate in the centre of the table.

"Anyone got any ideas?" Ballater asked the room.

Menzies gave a loud sniff. "Would I be speaking out of turn if I mentioned that the boss has always had a thing for Bobby's missus?"

"That doesn't exactly put him in a minority," Thomson said, keeping his eyes focused on the table rather than anyone seated around it.

"But now he gets to play the knight in shining armour," Menzies went on.

Ballater spaced his words out when he answered. "Are you saying you think the boss did Bobby in? I'm not convinced that would work out well for us."

"We need to be doing something, though," Paterson said, crumbs spraying from his parted lips.

"The Parlour's the obvious starting point," Ballater concluded after a moment's thought. "Pity we don't have any current friends inside the crime squad—a few rounds bought at the Top Spot could be helpful."

"Way I hear it, John Rhodes has his finger in that particular pie."

"And we don't get to Rhodes without going through his team first."

"Especially that big bastard with the face that looks like a join-the-dots painting."

"We're not exactly midgets ourselves, remember."

"Plenty of folk on the street we could be asking," Thomson said. "Word has a way of getting around."

"I dare say myths are being created as we sit here," Ballater added. "Soon enough we'll have to turn colliers to dig up anything resembling the truth."

"My dad was a coal miner," Thomson said.

"Let's hope his son doesn't have to take up a shovel or a pickaxe to find some answers."

Thomson gave a thin smile as he patted his jacket pocket. "There's only one tool I'll need, Mickey."

"Are youse still here?" Cam Colvin barked from the doorway, affecting incredulity as he wiped his hands dry on his handkerchief.

"Just going, chief," Paterson apologised, rising to his feet. He reached out an arm towards one final biscuit before thinking better of it and following his three colleagues from the room.

7

After Milligan's pre-lunch briefing, Laidlaw had felt the need not so much to clear his head as to exorcise the whole soul-festering hour. He'd jumped on a bus, no destination in mind, just staring from the top deck as the streets around him spun their endless small stories. He smoked cigarette after cigarette and thought of the Burleigh. If it was going to be his base camp for the duration, he needed to go home and pack some clothes. Ena wouldn't be happy about it, but that was increasingly becoming the default setting regarding their marriage. It felt as though they were living through a phoney war, negotiations fraught, hiding the truth from their civilian children. There were three of them—Moya, Sandra and Jack; aged six, five and two. Whenever a case kept him out past their bedtime, Laidlaw would creep into their rooms to stroke their hair and remind himself a better world was possible.

It wasn't so easy with Ena.

His thoughts shifted to the receptionist at the Burleigh. Her name was Jan, a well-upholstered woman with a steely stare that seemed to soften in Laidlaw's presence. He suspected that male admirers would wonder if they could pass whatever test she seemed to be setting with those eyes. She knew he was a detective because Ben Finlay had once told her to expect a visit.

"Nice to know I'm predictable."

"Ben seems to think you're anything but."

Laidlaw told himself that it wasn't Jan that kept him returning to the Burleigh; it was the need to stay near the steady pulse of the city streets. Simshill was too far, too safe. The kids needed stories told to them, meals were required to be eaten as a family. He was no longer supposed to be a policeman.

"You'll burn out before you're forty," Ena had once warned him.

Forty wasn't too far away, either. He felt it encircling his thickening waist. His knees complained when faced with too many stairs. His eyes were under strain and he doubted he could chase a suspect the length of any street worth the name. Wiping condensation from the bus window, he looked out at a sky belched from the chimneys of the crumbling tenements, the same smoke that clung to the various civic buildings, once grandly Victorian but now in danger of being swamped by modernity. Old habitats were being demolished, shiny towering replacements planned, a motorway carving its way through the city. Forget the old certitudes; they would soon be crushed underfoot like a fag end beneath a platform-soled shoe. Laidlaw didn't doubt, though, that the replenished housing stock would fail to do much for Glasgow's ingrained problems. Behind new glazing and harling he'd be sure still to find poverty, loveless marriages, drunken aggression, sectarian bile, like angry tattoos hidden under a laundered shirt.

He was only vaguely aware of his surroundings as he got off the bus at its next stop and crossed the road to await another back into town. The attempt to erase the memory of the briefing wasn't working. He was seeing Milligan standing in front of his attentive audience, never happier than when issuing orders and offering theories as if they were diamond-hard facts. A wall of black-and-white photographs acted as scenery to his soliloquy. One of them showed graffiti on the rear wall of the Parlour, left there by the Gorbals Cumbie, a teenage gang whose current leader was called Malky Chisholm.

Chisholm was a college dropout whose ambition of becoming a social worker had led him to too close an association with the various groupings of feral young men. It had become like a drug to him, and eventually, having attempted to broker peace between the Cumbie and other gangs such as the Calton Toi, he'd been offered no choice but to take sides. The Cumbie had become his tribe and soon enough he'd been crowned their king. It helped that he was a gifted amateur boxer. A "square go" held few fears for him—in a fair fight, he would almost always win. But he was cunning, too, meaning even unfair fights went his way.

Laidlaw was aware of a bit of history between Chisholm and Milligan. Arrests made; charges dropped. Milligan was strapping on a pair of blinkers to go with his boxing gloves, ready to enter the ring again.

"What this graffiti tells me," he had pontificated for the benefit of the room, "is that the Cumbie are encroaching on Calton turf. A stabbing is one hell of a calling card, wouldn't you agree?" His eyes had fixed on Laidlaw as he'd said this, as if daring him to shake his head. What would have been the point? The crime squad office was hardly the forum in Rome, and Laidlaw doubted anyone gathered there would have looked good in a toga. Ever since Lilley and Laidlaw had returned from the mortuary, Milligan had been waiting for them to complain that their trip there had been a waste of time. Neither man had done so, purely to deprive him of that pleasure.

Lighting another cigarette, Laidlaw became aware of a stooped old-timer with rheumy eyes who had joined the bus queue behind him.

"You should enjoy life more, son. Your face is tripping you."

The man's breath was like a blowtorch, and Laidlaw wondered why it was that after a drink so many Glaswegians turned into the Ancient Mariner, eager to share their stories and wisdom with complete strangers. This particular example boasted a rolled-up newspaper, which he wielded like a baton, as if he could conduct the world.

"At least it's only my face that's tripping me," Laidlaw responded. "Your whole life seems to be one long bout of falling over." He gestured towards the rips in the man's trousers and the elbows of his worn-out jacket.

The man studied him, taking a step back as if to help him focus. "You look like an actor, son. Have I seen you in anything?"

"We're all actors in this town, haven't you noticed? You're acting right now."

"Am I?"

"Badly—but even bad acting deserves the occasional round of applause." Laidlaw dug a few coins from his pocket and placed them in the man's hand. "Should cover your bus fare. Either that or a paper from this week rather than last."

There was a double-decker drawing towards them at that moment. Laidlaw gestured for the old man to precede him aboard, but then stood his ground and told the clippie he'd wait for the next one. The new passenger stared in bemusement from the window as the bell rang and the bus pulled away, depriving him of his audience. Laidlaw didn't doubt he would soon find another.

8

B ob Lilley was making show of studying the crime-scene photos when Ernie Milligan stopped in front of him. He smelled of Old Spice and ambition, neither of which particularly bothered Lilley, though he was an Aramis man himself. Milligan took a slurp of tea from a Mexico World Cup mug, which Lilley knew would be sweetened with the usual three sugars.

"Got enough to be getting on with?" he enquired.

Lilley decided to tickle his boss's belly. "Interesting what you said about the Cumbie. When do we talk to Chisholm?"

"Soon enough, Bob, don't you worry. Sorry about the post-mortem, by the way—crossed wires."

"You're bound to make a few mistakes along the way." Lilley watched Milligan's face stiffen. "I mean on a case as complex as this. Lot of plates spinning."

"Meantime your partner isn't so much a plate-spinner as a Harry Houdini."

"Is that what Laidlaw is, my partner? I get the feeling he'd object to the description. And to answer the question you're about to ask, I don't have a clue where he is. He hightailed it as soon as the briefing was done."

"Aye, and before I could dole out tasks."

"From what I've heard, Jack Laidlaw works best when left to his own devices."

"He needs reined in, Bob. That's your job."

"You want me tailing him around town?"

"I don't want him thinking he can set any agendas here, that's all." Milligan broke off as a WPC began Sellotaping a fresh set of photographs and clippings to the wall, including a snap of the deceased with his wife and children.

"Got that from the house," Milligan explained. "It's some place—you should see it. They've not long moved in. Decorators are still busy."

"How old's the photo?" Lilley leaned in towards it.

"Couple of years. Anniversary bash at the Albany. She's not changed much." Milligan's eyes were all over the widow. "She'll have suitors queuing up at her door."

"I'm assuming she'll be well provided for financially?"

"There's a will still to be read out, but you can bet there'll be money—not all of it within reach of the taxman, judging by the deceased's track record."

"Has the house been searched?"

"We didn't find a secret stash, if that's what you're asking."

"And Carter's office?"

"Under way. His secretary's helping between weeping fits." Milligan had noticed the Commander gesturing from the doorway. He nodded, placed the mug on the nearest desk and straightened his shoulders, but then paused for a moment. "Find Laidlaw. Keep me posted. Don't let him cloud your judgement. Oh, and make sure he's smoking and drinking plenty. I want him six feet under well before me. It's by way of a bet where the winner gets to dance a jig on the loser's grave."

Lilley watched Milligan march—actually march, arms swinging—towards the door. The phone on the desk behind him was ringing, so he picked it up.

"DS Lilley," he announced.

"I'm looking for Jack. Jack Laidlaw."

"He's not available at the moment. Can I take a message?"

"I'm his wife. Ena. Just wondered if I'd be seeing him today."

"You know he stayed at the Burleigh last night?"

"Not that he had the good grace to tell me himself, but I'd worked it out. You're on that murder case?"

"That's right, Ena."

"Sorry, I've forgotten your name already."

Lilley had rested his backside against a corner of the desk. "I'm Bob. Bob Lilley."

"I don't think he's mentioned you."

"Well, we've only recently been partnered." There was that word again.

"Good luck to you."

"I understand he can be a handful."

"Like saying Krakatoa gave off a bit of smoke." He could hear the smile in her voice. A tired smile, but still a smile. "Are you married, Bob?"

"Too long, my wife might say. We've a couple of grown kids."

"Lucky you—our three are going to be around for a while yet."

"I know that can be hard. Detectives tend to work unsociable hours at the best of times."

"And even when they're home, they're sometimes not home at all."

"You'd get no argument from my wife."

"Does she have a name?"

"Margaret."

"Maybe I should be swapping notes with her. Will you tell Jack I called?"

"Of course."

"Thank you."

Lilley was trying to work out what to say next, but the dialling tone told him she'd already ended the call.

9

The graffiti had been applied with an aerosol. Time was, a tin of paint and a brush would have been needed. Laidlaw was vague on how a gang named Cumbie had come to be associated with the Gorbals. Same went for the Tongs, the Spur and the Toi. They were part of a code, he supposed, and codes were not meant to be deciphered by everyone. Witness the Masonic handshake, which could be given without a non-believer being any the wiser. Not that a member of the craft would thank you for the comparison. It interested him that Lilley was not of the brotherhood; most cops felt obliged to join if they weren't already members. Quiet conversations had been had with Laidlaw early in his career, pointing out that it would be no detriment to advancement through the ranks. Quite the opposite, in fact, if he took the speaker's meaning. It was like the union hold over the working-class denizens of the shipyards and elsewhere: it wasn't mandatory to sign up and pay your dues, but if you didn't, there would always be mutterings that you weren't a team player.

Laidlaw suspected that this was what each gang conferred on its adherents, a sense of belonging, often where none had been nurtured at home. The other pieces of graffiti told their own stories, and the fact that derogatory comments had already been added alongside the word *Cumbie* told him that the message had been there a while, certainly long enough for the local gang to let the Cumbie know what they thought of this territorial slight. This was no new incursion or cry of intent. It was history. Soon enough it would be defaced entirely, a fresh layer of scrawls and scuffs covering it. Milligan, as ever, wasn't so much barking up the wrong tree as looking for a tree in the widest of oceans.

The bins next to where the body had lain had been emptied, their contents taken away to be sifted by specialists with more patience than Laidlaw. They probably enjoyed jigsaws of a rainy Sunday afternoon, too. A single bunch of flowers, shop-bought, sat in the gap between the bins. There was no note. As Laidlaw stood there contemplating, a gawker arrived, a man in a trench coat and NHS glasses, thin hair slicked back, wife a few steps behind him, happy to have her hero lead the way.

"Fuck right off," Laidlaw warned them both, as the man produced a cheap camera from his pocket.

"No harm in it," the man blurted out. But he had the decency to look ashamed as he turned and gave his wife a little shove. Laidlaw escorted them as far as the pavement, then, having waited a few moments, pushed open the door to the Parlour and headed in.

What greeted him was a frozen tableau, a moment captured for posterity. No one seated at any of the tables, four men standing at the bar, one having reached across to grab the landlord by his shirt front. All eyes were on Laidlaw as he entered. The shirt was released, the men adjusting their expressions.

"Thought you'd locked that," one growled softly to another.

"This the *University Challenge* audition?" Laidlaw enquired, approaching the bar. Then, to Conn Feeney specifically: "Bamber Gascoigne couldn't make it?"

One of the men jabbed a stubby finger towards him. "You leave here now, if you know what's good for you, pal."

"He's CID," another of the group piped up. "I can smell it from here."

Laidlaw took his time getting a cigarette lit. "You'll be Cam Colvin's boys," he commented. "If memory serves, that probably means one of you is called Panda."

"That's me," stated the one who'd smelled police on him.

"Yours is the only name I remember. That's how worried my lot are about you and your boss. You're barely specks of dust floating over a buckled tin ashtray." Laidlaw made show of tapping a finger against the ashtray in front of him. "Tin rather than glass because it's a lot less use in a fight. Ineffectual, you might even say. Look the word up when you get home—which is where I advise you to go right this second, before you start to really annoy me."

"This your idea of investigating a murder?" the one called Panda said. "Stopping off for a few free drinks and a smoke? We all know you won't be losing much sleep over Bobby, or breaking any sweat over the case."

"Problem is too many suspects," Laidlaw said. "I'd be as well opening the phone book and working my way through from the A's. What I *don't* need, however, is the likes of you doing my job for me, with threats and intimidation in place of a warrant card."

Panda didn't bother answering. He had become de facto leader, and his job now was to lead his men out of the pub with dignity intact.

"You'll be seeing us again," he shot towards the landlord. "Don't think you won't. Same goes for you, copper."

"The name's Laidlaw. Make sure that gets back to your boss. Write it down if you have to."

He watched them leave in silence. They walked in single file, repairing their swagger before facing the outside world. Feeney was jamming a glass under the nearest optic.

"You'll take one." It was more a demand than a question.

"I prefer Antiquary to the council stuff."

Feeney obliged, pouring liberally from a bottle. He added a

splash of water to his own, Laidlaw nodding to indicate that he'd have the same.

"Thanks for that," the landlord said.

"For what? They'll be back, just like they said. All the same, they've not managed to shake you up too much. I'm guessing that's because you've some Belfast blood in you."

"Born and bred."

"Lived through enough scares before you landed here?"

"A few." Feeney had already finished his drink but seemed in no hurry for another. He rinsed his glass and lit a cigarette of his own. "They're not exactly amateurs but they're not the worst I've seen."

"How about their boss?"

"Only known to me by reputation."

"And Bobby Carter?"

Feeney examined Laidlaw through the haze of smoke between them, his eyes narrowing slightly. "Okay, you've done me a good turn, so here's all I'm saying—he came in here once."

"Bobby Carter?"

"The same."

"You knew who he was?"

"Not at the time. After he left, one of my regulars enlightened me."

"That's why you recognised him in the alley." Laidlaw nodded his understanding. "So what was he doing here, the time he dropped in?"

"Waiting for someone to join him who never arrived."

"And you've no idea who?"

Feeney shook his head.

"He hadn't been in before?"

"No."

"So the pub was probably the other person's idea."

"If you say so."

"Meaning maybe someone you do know. Nobody ever asked if they'd missed him? Nobody arrived looking for him after he left?"

"Not to my knowledge."

"How long ago did all this happen?"

"Three or four weeks back."

"You should have told us."

"I'm telling you now. Don't make me regret it."

Laidlaw finished his drink and stubbed out the cigarette. He wrote the number of the Burleigh on a spare McEwan's coaster. "If you think of anything else," he said, sliding it across to Feeney. "Or if Colvin's men turn nasty."

"I can handle myself."

"Thing is, you probably have limits, boundaries you won't cross because your conscience won't allow it. These men don't. You'd be wise to bear that in mind."

Laidlaw walked to the door, hauled it open and stepped outside, coming face to face with two men, one of them John Rhodes. Rhodes was tall and fair-haired, not overly heavy in build. His face was pockmarked and had been since borstal days, though no one ever commented on the fact. His eyes were blue and often had a smile playing around them, as now. The man at his shoulder had a heavily scarred face and what looked like a permanent scowl, his eyes as animated as mortar shells.

"Jack Laidlaw," Rhodes said, sliding his hands into his pockets as if getting comfortable.

"Hello, John. Whatever in the world brings you here?"

"I like to know what's happening in my neck of the woods."

"You just missed some of Cam Colvin's men."

"Well isn't that lucky for them?" He glanced past Laidlaw towards the bar. "Any damage?"

"Landlord seemed to be coping."

"I don't doubt it."

"Is this one of your properties?" Laidlaw watched Rhodes shake his head. "Your visit here might suggest otherwise to Colvin."

"If I was going to take out Colvin's consigliere, I'd hardly have dumped him on my own patch. Not even your colleagues could be that dense—unless of course Milligan's in charge." Rhodes's smile widened when he saw Laidlaw's face tighten a fraction. "He is, though? Wonderful . . ."

"What did you mean by consigliere?"

"Have you not seen *The Godfather* yet? Get your arse to a picture house while it's still playing. It's a name for a right-hand man, the kind with a brain worth listening to. Now that Carter's been written off, Colvin's short of ready replacements."

"So someone took Carter out to knock the foundations from under Colvin? That would be a smart move, the kind a man like John Rhodes might make."

"Aye, or Matt Mason, or one of half a dozen other names we could bandy about all afternoon."

"Should I maybe add Malky Chisholm to the mix?"

"His lot are nothing more than toerags, Jack, you know that as well as I do." Rhodes's eyes widened a little. "Christ, is that the angle Milligan's taking? The bugger's thicker than the doorstop on a plain loaf."

"Doesn't mean he doesn't sometimes get a result, fluke or no. Have we got a bit of gang warfare to look forward to, John?"

"You'd have to ask Colvin. Me, I'm just a concerned citizen and businessman." Rhodes pressed his hands to his chest, hands that had throttled the life from men and picked up clubs and axes to be wielded against others, maybe even pressed a gun to a forehead or jaw. "I'll see you around, Jack. Regards to Ena . . ."

Laidlaw was in two minds about following, but he didn't think Rhodes would appreciate the company. His minder headed indoors with a final scowl in Laidlaw's direction. A pair of denim-clad men in their early twenties had been watching from across the street. They now crossed, hesitating just shy of the door.

"Was that who we think it was?" one asked. Laidlaw nodded his response. The speaker turned to his companion. "We'll maybe try the Sarry Heid instead, then."

Laidlaw almost asked if he could join them. But instead he flagged down a passing taxi and climbed in.

"Did you hear what happened behind that pub, son?" the driver shouted above the noise of the overworked engine.

"A family lost a husband and father," Laidlaw said. "That's what happened. Now give me a bit of peace, will you? I need to do some thinking."

Conn Feeney locked the doors of the Parlour and joined John Rhodes in the cramped back office, leaving Rhodes's bodyguard perched on a stool at the bar. Rhodes had made himself comfortable on the only chair and was sifting through the paperwork scattered across the desk, the same antique desk he had gifted Feeney on the day he'd taken ownership of the pub, praising its solidity.

"Belonged to a bank manager," he'd said. "I've checked down the back of the drawers but he didn't leave anything."

"You're sure I can't offer you something, John?" Feeney asked now, taking up position just inside the doorway. The room was windowless and consequently airless. Rhodes's aftershave filled it.

"I hear you had a visit, Conn."

"Cam Colvin's boys."

"I suppose that's to be expected," Rhodes mused. "If you need a bit of protection in the short term, you only have to ask."

"I'll be fine, John."

"Police give you any grief?"

"If you're meaning that guy Laidlaw, the answer's no."

"They'll know I've got a share in this place, though, eh?"

"If they do, they didn't hear it from me."

Rhodes nodded slowly, seemingly only half listening. One polished shoe tapped against the old green safe that sat on the floor alongside the desk. It, too, had come from a shutdown bank. "I need something, Conn," he said.

Feeney didn't need telling twice. He took the key from his trouser pocket and squatted in front of the safe, unlocking it and turning the handle. The safe contained some papers, a dozen thick bundles of banknotes, and a small muslin-wrapped object. That object had made its way to Glasgow from Belfast, courtesy of someone Conn had known back in the day. Today, however, Rhodes was interested only in the cash, peeling a few notes from one of the bundles and slipping them into his jacket. Feeney knew that almost every establishment linked to John Rhodes had a safe like this. The man spread his money around, feeling this to be a safer option than storing it all in the one place.

And he didn't trust the banking system, seeing it as the tax-man's snitch.

Having pocketed the money, however, he did allow his eyes to settle on the little muslin package.

"It's there if you need it," he said in a voice lacking all emotion.

"I know that, John."

Rhodes nodded to himself and patted his jacket, satisfying himself that the banknotes were safe within.

Conn Feeney took this as his cue to relock the safe.

"Maybe a drink now, eh?" Rhodes said. It was a mark of the man that he even made it sound like a suggestion rather than an order.

Ena Laidlaw was in the kitchen, keeping an eye on the twin-tub washing machine. Left to its own devices, the waste hose had a habit of unhooking itself from the side of the sink, sending water spewing across the linoleum floor. The pulley was already full from the previous load. This one would have to go on the clothes horse in front of the fire. Moya and Sandra were at school, Jack Junior parked on the sofa with an army of toy soldiers. Most of the washing seemed to be his. Give him sweets, chocolate or a lolly and some of it would end up on cardigan, shirt and trousers. The brown carpet in the living room had turned out to be a blessing of sorts, covering a multitude of stains.

She thought of how nice Bob Lilley had sounded on the phone. Not abrupt or wary like some detectives she'd had to call in the past. Their various stories always sounded fake or rehearsed—he's on his way to court or Barlinnie; he's in a meeting; he's gone to the records office.

You know he stayed at the Burleigh last night? Just like that, without her having to ask. And then offering up that he had kids of his own and a wife called . . . Margaret? That was it: Margaret. Margaret Lilley, who sounded like she had the measure of her husband.

Maybe I should be swapping notes with her.

"Maybe I should at that," Ena said quietly to herself, before realising that Jack Junior was standing in the doorway, an orange in his hand, juice soaking into his pullover and a sour look on his face. He had bitten into it through the thick skin.

"I told you," she said with a sigh. "But would you take a telling?"

She had taken a couple of steps towards him when her senses alerted her to the waste hose wriggling free of its perch.

"No you don't, mister," she said, giving it a firm push with one hand as she reached with the other towards a rinsed dish-cloth. In her mind she could see the telephone stool in the hall.

There was a little book there next to the phone, containing addresses and numbers of friends and family. And on a shelf beneath sat the Glasgow directory, which just might have a number in it for R. Lilley or M. Lilley or even R. and M. Lilley. Once the washing was hung up, she'd boil the kettle, settle down next to Jack Junior, and he could help her look.

10

L aidlaw was at a corner table in the Top Spot. A pint was waiting for Bob Lilley but it had already gone flat, and he pushed it aside as he arrived and sat down. Laidlaw folded closed the newspaper he'd been reading.

"What's happening in the world?" Lilley asked.

"Fighting in Belfast and peace at Upper Clyde. Plus my Premium Bonds mean I have to keep working." His eyes met Lilley's. "Thought you were standing me up."

"Much as I'd like to be able to rush from a murder case whenever summoned by someone who's taken up residence in a bar . . ." Lilley glanced towards the barman, who had made the call on Laidlaw's behalf.

"Thing is, Bob, you'd have been rushing *to* a murder case. This is where it's going to get solved."

"The Top Spot?"

"The streets," Laidlaw corrected him. "Sitting at a desk sucks all the oxygen out of you. That's maybe somebody's idea of policing, but not mine. I'm good at this city, though. I would definitely make that claim. It's because I keep doing my homework. You going to drink that?" When Lilley shook his head, Laidlaw poured half the stale pint into the remains of his own. "You can do deductive reasoning anywhere, but sometimes an office is the worst place for it, especially with Milligan nipping your napper."

"So what exactly have you deduced?"

"Remind me, what was in the victim's pockets when they were searched?"

"Apart from the cash—wallet, house keys, cigarettes and a fancy lighter. Nice wristwatch on him, too."

"So we can assume whoever killed him didn't do it in the act of robbing him?"

"Unless they panicked."

Laidlaw was shaking his head. "A gang like the Cumbie, they'd have picked the carcass clean."

"Meaning Milligan's wasting his time?"

"And everyone's hard graft to boot. But to come back to the vultures, Bobby Carter had been missing the best part of three days. You reckon he was lying there all that time without someone noticing? From the amount of graffiti, I'd say that lane's a popular enough spot, maybe for a drug deal or underage drinking, or even a knee-trembler like the one that eventually saw Carter found."

"You're saying the body was moved?"

"If the autopsy's right and he'd been dead two to three days, yes, I'm saying the body was moved."

"Why, though? And where from?"

Laidlaw did no more than shrug. "Landlord told me in confidence that Carter had been in just the one time, meeting someone who never arrived. I'd be surprised if there wasn't a connection. I just can't see what it is yet." He pinched the bridge of his nose.

"You okay?"

"I get migraines—and that's to be treated confidentially, too. Think one might just be trying to book an appointment."

"Seen a doctor about it?"

"I've got tablets."

"Do they work?"

"When added to ten or twelve hours on a bed in a darkened room."

"You should let Milligan know."

"Why?"

"Good excuse for when you go off wandering."

"But also a sign of weakness. I'd rather not give him any more ammunition. How about you—any progress to report?"

"Not as such. Your wife rang, though. Wanted to know if she'd be seeing you tonight. She sounds nice."

"She's great."

"The sort of woman a man would be happy to go home to?" Lilley had lifted what was left of his pint and taken an exploratory sip.

"I can get you a fresh one."

"In place of an answer to my question?"

Laidlaw couldn't help the thin smile. He took a deep breath. "Like I say, Ena is great. It's just that not much else is."

"Being a parent is hard work."

"Ach, it's not that." He looked to the gaudily painted ceiling for inspiration. "I'm lonelier in my marriage than when I lived on my own, and I think Ena's the same."

The silence at the table was deep enough to accommodate a coffin. Eventually it was broken by the bar's jukebox. Someone had put on 'Ain't No Sunshine.' The two detectives' eyes met and they shared a battle-worn smile. A shambling figure was approaching from the bar, holding a pint of Guinness in one hand and what looked like a large dark rum in the other.

"Hope it's okay, Mr. Laidlaw. I said you'd settle up later." The man sat down without waiting to be asked.

"This is Eck Adamson," Laidlaw said by way of introduction. A rich bouquet of aromas reached Lilley, courtesy of the new arrival in the greasy, ill-fitting clothes. There were old shaving cuts between the patches of bristle on his chin and cheeks. The hair was sparse and prematurely silver. Adamson could have been anything between thirty and sixty and probably had no more than a decade left in him without a radical change of lifestyle. "I told you I know the streets," Laidlaw was saying, "but Eck here has a doctorate and any number of diplomas."

As if in agreement with this assessment, Adamson toasted the table before sinking the rum in a single full-mouthed swallow. After a moment's exhalation, he started making short work of the pint.

"As you can see," Laidlaw went on, "all that expertise doesn't come cheap. But I can always rely on Eck, because he knows that if I think he's not earned the outlay, he's going to get a boot to the balls and a smack to the jaw." His words froze Adamson mid gulp. With infinite deliberation he placed the Guinness back on the table.

"Ernie Milligan reckons he's got the best sources in the city," Lilley commented, eliciting a snort of derision from Adamson.

"You mean Macey?"

"Benny Mason, yes."

"That's his Sunday name—and let me tell you, Macey's about as much use as brewer's droop at an orgy."

"Been to many orgies, have you?" Lilley was smiling without humour.

"I get plenty, don't you worry."

Laidlaw leaned across the table. "Eck, you couldn't get a ride in a brothel with a hundred quid and a doctor's line, but if I thought Macey had better ears it'd be him sitting there while you were curled up on the pavement next to a heating vent. So tell us what you've heard and I might even offer you a refill."

It was Adamson's turn to lean in, elbows on the table, as if ensuring his words remained the property of no one else in the bar.

"He wasn't the worst of men, Bobby Carter. Always stood his round as well as his ground."

"It's not a eulogy I'm after, Eck." Laidlaw's look was stern.

"I'm just setting the scene. Thing is, all men have vices and weak spots, don't they? With Carter it was women. I think hanging out with Colvin and the like only made things worse.

He got the feeling women were paying him attention because they liked him rather than because of the company he was in and the money flying around." Adamson reckoned he was safe to pause long enough for a sip from his glass. On the other side of the table Laidlaw mirrored him.

"So he was a womaniser," Lilley said across the no-man's-land. "So what?"

Adamson held up a finger whose entrenched stains Swarfega would struggle to overcome. "One woman," he intoned.

"Doubtless unmarried and with no other complications?" Laidlaw enquired.

"Chick McAllister's ex."

"Chick McAllister as in John Rhodes's Chick McAllister?"

"The same."

"Was this public knowledge?"

"If it was, you wouldn't need me to tell you."

"So who knew? Did McAllister?"

"Maybe. But they split up last year, amicably as far as I know."

"She seeing anyone apart from Carter?"

Adamson gave a shrug before sucking the last of the life from the Guinness. Laidlaw clicked his fingers towards the underworked barman, signalling for refills.

"So what's she called?"

"Jennifer Love. Goes by Jenni with an i. Sounds like an alias but it's genuine. Her dad's Archie Love, the footballer."

"I know that name," Lilley said. "There was a betting scandal, wasn't there?"

Adamson nodded. "And that was the end of his playing days. Since then he's been drinking to forget."

"What else do you know about Jenni?"

"Mid twenties. Likes a good time and men who can afford to bring her it on a plate. Works as a go-go dancer at Whiskies. It's that live music place on Candleriggs."

"A haunt of yours, I'm sure," Laidlaw said, breaking off as

the drinks arrived. There was one for Lilley, which he was determined to leave untouched. Again Adamson knocked back the rum in one swallow.

"Keeps the chill off," he explained.

"So will this," Laidlaw said, slipping him a banknote, which Adamson palmed like an expert. "Any other news for us while we're being cosy and friendly?"

"The drums are spelling out war, but that probably won't come as a surprise."

"Colvin looking for revenge?"

"Someone's going to have to pay. The pub where they found the body, it's on Rhodes's turf."

"I spotted him there not two hours ago," Laidlaw agreed, eliciting a look from Lilley.

"Story is, Rhodes and the owner go back a ways. Guy had to get out of Belfast in a hurry and Rhodes lent a hand, maybe even got him the shipyard job. Then the guy scoops the pools and buys the Parlour, even after splitting the winnings with Rhodes as a thank you."

"So if Colvin goes ruffling feathers there . . ." Laidlaw locked eyes with Lilley to make sure he understood the implications before turning his attention back to Adamson.

"Why was he killed, though, Eck? That's what we need to find out."

"*Cherchez la femme*, that's what they say, Mr. Laidlaw."

"And you wouldn't have been paid a princely sum by anyone to lead us into that particular maze?"

Adamson managed to look insulted, even as he sank half of the fresh pint of Guinness. He wiped foam from his top lip as he shook his head.

"Because if I find out you've been trying to play us," Laidlaw continued calmly, "it won't be your balls I'll be kicking into powder—it'll be that shrivelled thing inside you that passes for a soul."

11

L illey offered him a lift home and Laidlaw decided not to refuse. But he did ask for a detour, giving the address in Bearsden, and when Lilley asked why, all he could do was shrug.

"You saw John Rhodes," Lilley said. "When were you going to tell me that?"

"I literally bumped into him as I was coming out of the Parlour, just after I'd walked in on Colvin's goons giving the landlord some grief." Laidlaw paused, eyes on the passing scenery. "Lucky the two opposing forces didn't meet."

"And this is your normal way of working?"

"It's the only way I know."

"Seems to me, every station you work at, that method only gets you so far before you've put everyone's back up and have to be shunted elsewhere."

"What is it they say about a prophet in his own country?"

"That he should start making allies, because one day he might just need them?"

"Aye, something like that." Laidlaw reached down to switch on the radio. Dr. Kissinger was talking about peace in Vietnam. "They'd be as well sending Dr. Strangelove," Laidlaw commented.

"You reckon Nixon's going to beat McGovern next month?"

"*I* could beat McGovern, Bob. Every time I think politics here can't get any lower or more venal, I look across the pond and wonder if I'm staring into a crystal ball."

"Kissinger's got a head on him, though."

"Aye, and if it gets any bigger he'll have trouble squeezing through the doors of all those planes he seems to like taking. Say what you like about the Scots, we hate to see people get above themselves."

"We're all Jock Tamson's bairns right enough."

"And what a bastard of a father he turned out to be . . ."

"This'll do," Laidlaw stated when they reached Bobby Carter's street.

"We going in?"

Laidlaw shook his head. The car had stopped one house shy of Carter's. Time was, mourning meant the curtains would be drawn closed day and night until after the funeral, but he got the feeling the downstairs ones had been pulled to only because it had grown dark.

"She's a bit of a looker, the widow," Lilley stated. "Milligan has a photo up on the murder wall. I'd say he's slightly smitten. Wonder how she ended up with a piece of pond life like Bobby Carter."

Laidlaw drew in a deep breath. "When me or my brother were bad-mouthing someone, our mum always said the same thing—'Ach, he's somebody's rearing.' I suppose what she meant was, everyone's loved by someone and we don't always know the reason why."

"You're telling me even arseholes have their good side and deserve some sort of justice?"

"The law's not about justice. It's a system we've put in place because we can't have justice."

Lilley thought: the man speaks like the books on his desk, the lines honed by rehearsal. But did they mean much of anything?

Laidlaw was winding down the window, nodding towards the lamplit suburban street. "This is why we have to solve the case," he said. "On the surface everything appears much as it was, but one house has been hit by a bomb. They're in there sifting through the rubble. Carter might have been a mobster outside the home, but here he was a husband and dad. That's our client, Bob—Dr. Jekyll rather than Mr. Hyde."

"Wonder if the rest of the street knew how he came to afford a home here."

They noticed movement at the living room window of the house opposite the Carters' and caught a glimpse of an elderly face. Whoever was inside was pretending to adjust the curtains while actually wondering whose car had just arrived.

"Nosy parker," Lilley stated.

"The neighbourhood eyes and ears," Laidlaw agreed.

"So we're not going in and we're not getting out?"

"We're travellers, Bob, that's all."

"Aye, and some of us want to travel home. Others I'm not so sure about."

"Did you sign up thinking the job was nine to five?"

"They told me ten till four with regular breaks."

"Maybe that's my problem then—I should have joined the union as well as the lodge. But if you're in a hurry, I've seen what I need to."

"And what's that?"

"Another piece of the infinite jigsaw that makes Glasgow the second city of the Empire."

Lilley was shaking his head slowly as he executed a three-point turn, wondering if working with Laidlaw was likely to get any easier.

Laidlaw himself started giving directions as they reached the outskirts of Simshill. His home was on a street between Linn Park and King's Park. Lilley didn't know the area and would probably have called it Cathcart rather than Simshill. Without being asked, he had informed Laidlaw that he and Margaret had lived in Dowanhill all their married lives and he couldn't see them flitting any time soon.

"I've brought you out of your way," Laidlaw said, almost apologetically.

"Which means I can take you back, if you want me to wait."

He shook his head. "Might take a bit of time to pack. I'll be fine in a taxi."

As they drew to a stop, the door of the semi-detached house opened, as if Ena had been waiting. When Laidlaw emerged from the car, Lilley got out too. He stood at the driver's side and offered a smile in her direction, which she answered with a wave. She was a handsome woman but looked fatigued. Laidlaw's shoulders were hunched as he walked up the path towards her. If the visit to Bearsden had energised him, that energy had now dissipated, though he revived when one of his children bounded past her mother and hurled herself into Laidlaw's arms.

Lilley felt all of a sudden that he was intruding on a private moment, albeit one played out in public view. He dived back into the car and put it into gear. His last view was of Laidlaw's back, the child's thin arms clamped around his neck as both headed indoors. Ena had already left the stage.

It was ten by the time Laidlaw stepped out of the taxi at the Burleigh Hotel. The driver hadn't felt much like chatting after Laidlaw had asked which of the city's gangsters he ultimately worked for. Cabs, scrapyards, bouncers, knocking shops, betting offices—scratch the surface of any of those industries and you'd find a Rhodes, a Colvin or a Matt Mason. When he'd added a tip to the fare, there had been the most token grunt of gratitude, so much so that he'd almost asked for it back. Instead, he'd picked up his case and pushed open the door to the hotel, climbing the three steps to the reception desk, where Jan greeted him with a welcoming smile.

"Hello, stranger."

"Wasn't I just here last night?"

"Feels longer." She had opened her ledger and was studying it. "Can't offer you the same room—it's taken. Guy's here on business, but for one night only. How about I give you the suite tonight and you can move tomorrow?"

"How much is the suite?"

"No extra charge."

"Money up front?"

She shook her head. "I know you're not going to run out on me." She turned towards the row of numbered hooks. "Just the one key, or will anyone be joining you?"

"About ten other versions of me, none of whose company I can honestly say I enjoy." He took the key from her, eye contact lasting only slightly longer than strictly necessary.

"Well, if you need anything, you know where to find me."

"You always work the late shift?"

"I like being awake at night. There's the feeling that anything could happen."

"Out there it usually does." Laidlaw gestured to the door behind him.

"And in here too sometimes."

"Second floor?" He was making show of studying the red-tasselled key.

"Third. There are only two rooms up there and the other's not taken yet, so you can make as much noise as you want."

He got the feeling she was smiling again as he made his way towards the lift.

DAY THREE

12

L aidlaw was eating a cooked breakfast in the dining room when the day-shift receptionist handed him a message, apologising for her scrawled writing. It took him a couple of attempts to work out that it was from Conn Feeney. Carter's widow was due to visit the scene of the crime before saying a few words to some tame journalists. Laidlaw didn't bother mopping up the last of the fried egg. He slipped his jacket on and got going.

By the time he reached the Parlour, things were drawing to a close. The press photographers were taking a few final snaps. Neighbours and passers-by formed an appreciative audience on the pavement across from where Monica Carter stood, dressed in sober colours, her naturally pale face lacking any adornment, yet still striking, hair tied back, eyes misty. Two print journalists—neither of them familiar to Laidlaw—were checking their notepads in case they'd missed anything. Next to the widow stood a figure Laidlaw did recognise—Cam Colvin. He wasn't wearing a suit as such, but both jacket and trousers were dark, as was his tie. Laidlaw doubted any of it had come from Milligan's favoured menswear shop. One hand held Monica Carter's elbow while she finished whatever she was telling the press.

Laidlaw was reminded of the pathologist's words. He'd said Colvin had "handled her with great gentleness." And here he was handling her again, head bowed but eyes like darts aimed at the reporters, warning them not to overstep the mark. His shoulders were slightly hunched, the result of the knife in the back that had become part of the city's mythology. Laidlaw noticed that Colvin's free hand was twisted almost behind his back. He was holding something there. Laidlaw moved further to the edge of the throng. It was the posy from behind the pub. Colvin had removed it for some reason.

Laidlaw scratched his jaw, realising he hadn't shaved that morning. He kept watching as Colvin decided enough was enough. No, Mrs. Carter would not be posing for a few tasteful portraits. No, she wouldn't be sitting down for any private confab. The journalists were shooed away as a car drew to a halt, driven by one of the men Laidlaw had bearded in the Parlour. Colvin himself ushered the widow into the back seat, settling next to her. As the car drew away, normality returned, as if the curtain had come down at the end of a performance. Laidlaw saw that the door to the Parlour was slightly open, Conn Feeney watching through the gap. He gave the landlord a thumbs-up of thanks for the tip-off. Rather than acknowledge it, Feeney simply let the door swing closed. Opening time wouldn't be for a while yet.

Laidlaw wasn't the only onlooker who made the pilgrimage to the bins behind the pub. A couple of permed housewives in Rainmates and what looked like floral dressing gowns were ahead of him. One stooped to study the writing on the large bunch of fresh flowers.

"They're beauties," her friend said.

"From your wife and loving children," the other woman recited. Then, to Laidlaw: "I hope you're not thinking of nicking them."

"I'm not," he assured her. But he did wonder about the other flowers, the ones Colvin had decided didn't belong.

"Such a waste," the first woman said. Laidlaw wondered whether she meant the loss of human or horticultural life.

As the two women shuffled off, he lit a cigarette and read

the inscription for himself. Over a dozen blooms rested behind the cellophane wrapping, already dead but making the best of it, which in itself wasn't the worst of epitaphs.

Milligan was just finishing the morning briefing when Laidlaw walked into the office.

"Nice of you to join us, Jack."

"I've been listening from the corridor—didn't want to interrupt your flow."

"Then you'll know what duties you and Bob have been assigned?"

"Absolutely." Laidlaw pulled out his chair and sat down. There was a mound of fresh paperwork on his desk. The typing pool had been busy. Bob Lilley was studying his own copies, managing to avoid eye contact with his partner.

Milligan clapped his hands together twice. "Let's get busy then."

As the detectives roused themselves, Milligan began to move towards Laidlaw's desk, but a WPC appeared in the doorway and announced that the Commander wanted a word. With a glower towards Laidlaw that warned of unfinished business, Milligan made his exit, straightening his tie as he went.

"So what *are* our duties?" Laidlaw asked Lilley.

"I thought you knew."

"Let's pretend I arrived at the station five minutes ago after a return visit to the Parlour."

"It opens early."

"I had a tip-off. Watched the widow and Cam Colvin talking to some journalists after leaving a bouquet. Colvin's the type of gangster who likes to see his photo in the paper—means more of his fellow Glaswegians know who they're supposed to fear. Recognition and reputation are all."

"So you got a good look at Carter's wife then? Can I add you to the list of the smitten?"

"How about you tell me what intellectual challenge we've been set for the rest of the day?"

"We're on door-to-door."

"The CID equivalent of jankers, in other words."

"Milligan's pulling Malky Chisholm in for questioning but saving that for himself."

"While we waste a solid day asking the deaf, dumb and blind if they've seen or heard anything suspicious."

"I take it you have a better idea?"

"Only if you've yet to mention Jennifer Love to anyone."

"I kept that under my hat."

"Any particular reason why?"

"Eck Adamson is your snitch, meaning you should be the one given the honour."

"Decent of you, but that same decency might see you stuck at DS for longer than necessary. Stealing your colleagues' glory is a tried-and-tested shortcut to advancement."

"I've always preferred scenic routes myself."

"Then this is your lucky day, DS Lilley."

"Whiskies go-go bar?" Lilley guessed.

"Whiskies go-go bar," Laidlaw echoed, shoving the paperwork to the furthest corner of his desk.

Though the club wouldn't open for hours, staff were already busy cleaning and restocking. There was an aroma of musky sweat and spilled beer that had not yet been disguised by the cans of deodoriser. Small circular podiums, each with a chrome pole at its centre, stood at the four corners of the dance floor. Laidlaw visualised Jenni Love gyrating as the ceiling-mounted spotlights played over her body. The owner of Whiskies, a man named Jake Collins, wasn't in yet, but the self-styled "bar manager," a bleary-eyed teenager with raging acne and home-made tattoos, reckoned he could help them with an address for Jenni. As he headed to the back office,

Laidlaw signalled for Lilley to accompany him. Last thing they wanted was Love being telephoned a warning. In Lilley's absence, Laidlaw walked to the DJ booth. It boasted two record decks and a cassette player plus a control panel for the lights. A reel-to-reel sat on the floor, apparently considered obsolete. Promotional photos, their curling edges showing their age, were pinned to the booth's back wall. Laidlaw recognised a few faces: Marmalade, Lulu, Cilla.

"She sang in here once, you know," a voice called from the bar. Laidlaw turned towards the man who was unloading bottles from a crate. He was in his thirties. Sleeves rolled up, stomach bulging, a sheen of sweat on his face. "Lulu, I mean. Back before this place became Whiskies. Everyone from the Corries to the Poets passed through those doors."

"Not these days, though?"

"Dancing's what works up a thirst, and a DJ doesn't cost what a proper musician does."

Laidlaw made show of studying his surroundings. "Who owns the place now?"

"Jake Collins."

"Aye, on paper maybe. But who's pulling his strings? Cam Colvin?"

"I've no idea."

"Your face says otherwise. Ever see Bobby Carter in here?"

"The guy who was killed?" The man decided not to bother lying. "He came in now and again."

"With Colvin?" A shake of the head. "And I'm guessing not with his wife?"

"You're getting Jenni's address, so I'm assuming you already know."

"I don't suppose you ever saw her ex in here, name of Chick McAllister?"

Another shake of the head, more definitive this time. The man concentrated on emptying the crate and readying the next one. Bob Lilley was emerging from the back office, flourishing a scrap of paper, the teenager at his heels.

Laidlaw gestured towards both employees. "If she's flown the nest, we'll be straight back here and you'll be spending some time in the cells at Central Division. Enjoy the rest of your day, gents."

13

J ennifer Love still lived at home with her parents. It was her
mother who opened the door of the bungalow in
Knightswood. The area was undergoing development, new
tower blocks beginning to appear. In time they might swamp
the existing housing altogether, smothering the life out of it.
Jennifer was still in bed, Laidlaw and Lilley were informed.
They knew what young people were like these days. Her
mother would see if she could be roused. Mrs. Love led them
down the narrow hallway, past a venerable-looking paraffin
heater, into the living room, where a coal fire was sparking and
spitting, the fireside itself immaculate. Did they want tea or
coffee? Was anything wrong?

"Just a couple of questions about someone she might know,"
Bob Lilley explained.

"And who might that be?"

"Bobby Carter."

The woman's lips puckered but she held her counsel.

"Your face gives you away, Mrs. Love," Laidlaw said. "So if
you were thinking of trying to hide anything from us, I'd advise
against."

She folded her arms slowly while she debated silently with
herself.

"Jennifer spilled the beans to me," she eventually admitted.
"Not at the start, but soon enough after. And him a married
man, too. But they'd stopped seeing one another. It was never
that serious. I don't think they even . . ." She broke off, giving

her permed hair a pat as if to tidy it. "Anyway, I'll go fetch her."

They waited in the living room. It was festooned with memorabilia from Archie Love's playing days. Morton, Dunfermline, then a short unsuccessful spell at Rangers before seeing out his professional days at St. Johnstone. There were trophies and medals, a cap from his one outing for the national team, and framed photos of him posing with everyone from Jim Baxter to Jock Stein, Hamish Imlach to Molly Weir. Other photos showed a young boy. One of these seemed to have been cropped from a larger picture, the edges rough. It sat next to a family portrait, posed in a studio, the photographer's name embossed along the bottom of the white cardboard frame. Love looked every inch the patriarch. His wife was just about managing a smile, while Jennifer, aged probably eleven or twelve, was showing signs that she was present under sufferance and sufferance alone.

When Mrs. Love returned, she told them Jennifer would be a couple of minutes. She was readying to sit down, but Laidlaw informed her they needed a bit of privacy. Her face hardened.

"I'll be in the kitchen then." There was no follow-up offer of beverages.

"Your husband's not here?" Lilley enquired.

"He runs a youth team. They keep him busy." She left the room.

The two men sat in silence, side by side on the sofa. Archie Love's armchair held a cleaned ashtray and a spectacles case. The chair looked well used and Laidlaw guessed the man in the photographs had put on weight since his heyday. His wife was a sparrow by comparison, albeit one that would protect her nest to the death. Jennifer Love, when she entered, had many of her mother's delicate features, but with added height and looks. Her dark hair was shoulder length, her eyes lucid and watchful. She settled in what would be her mother's usual chair, tucking her legs beneath her. Mid twenties and still living with mum and dad—Laidlaw wondered who stood to gain most from the arrangement.

"We'd stopped seeing each other," she announced.

"All the same, we're sorry for your loss."

She bit her bottom lip, as if realising she should be showing a sorrow that wasn't there.

"When was the last time you saw Mr. Carter?" Lilley asked.

"Couple of weeks back."

"Was this at Whiskies?" Lilley watched her nod. "He was a regular?"

"If I was dancing, yes."

"Is that how you met?"

"Yes."

Laidlaw leaned towards her, his elbows resting on his knees. "And what caused the split?" he asked.

"Nothing really."

"You'd made it clear to him you weren't going to share a bed?"

Her eyes widened a little at the question's lack of subtlety.

"Sorry to be so blunt, Jenni," he went on, "but this is a murder inquiry."

She nodded again, this time in understanding. "I think we just didn't have enough in common. He didn't even like the music at the club. He just liked ogling the girls."

"He was generous, though—always buying the drinks? A meal now and then? Maybe a bit of jewellery?"

"Yes."

"You must have known something would be expected in return. The guy was married. There was a reason he was with you rather than his wife."

"I suppose so."

"What about Cam Colvin? Ever see him at Whiskies?"

"I never met him, but Bobby talked about him all the time. I think I was supposed to find that whole world as exciting as he did."

"You've got a head on your shoulders," Laidlaw said. "That's something you should be proud of." He paused, allowing her a moment to inhale the praise. "What about your old boyfriend Chick?"

"What about him?"

"Was he jealous you were seeing Bobby?"

She offered a shrug. "Haven't seen Chick in months."

"How many months?"

"Two, maybe three."

"Did he know about you and Bobby, though?"

"Not many people did. We were discreet."

"Not easy in a city of a million eyes. So is there any reason you can think of why someone would want Bobby dead?"

"Apart from the fact he worked for a gangster?"

"How about the Parlour—did he ever take you there, or mention it?"

She shook her head. She was dressed in black slacks, her feet bare, and she had begun to pick at a toenail, as if seeking a distraction.

"Is there anything you *can* tell us about Bobby?" Laidlaw persisted. "Anything that might help us catch his killer?"

"He just seemed like every other lawyer. A bit quiet, a bit boring, truth be told. But I knew part of his job was storing other people's secrets. You always felt he was working hard at not letting anything slip."

"And these secrets, did you get any inkling where he was storing them?"

She saw that Laidlaw had misunderstood. "Up here," she explained, tapping her forehead.

Bob Lilley cleared his throat, signalling that he had a question of his own. "Are you sorry he's dead, Jenni?"

"Of course I am. Can't go weeping and wailing, though, can I?"

"You left a bunch of flowers behind the Parlour, didn't

you?" Laidlaw added. He watched her nod slowly. "No name or card . . . I'm guessing Bobby was a secret kept between you and your mother?"

Jennifer Love looked around the room she was sitting in. "Dad would have hit the roof."

"There's no way he could have found out?"

"I'd know all about it if he had, believe me."

"But supposing he had, he would be far from best pleased?"

"He's a hard man to please at any time."

There was the sound of a stifled sneeze from the other side of the living room door.

"We're almost done, Mrs. Love," Laidlaw announced, raising his voice. "You can come in if you like."

By the time he reached the hallway, however, Jenni's mother was back at the kitchen sink and refusing to lift her eyes from whatever lurked in her washing-up bowl.

"You'll find whoever killed him?" Bob Lilley was being asked.

"Don't you worry about that," Lilley replied in practised tones, before following Laidlaw to the front door.

Seated in Lilley's Toledo, Laidlaw got a cigarette going. "Archie Love?" Lilley speculated.

"We'll take it to Milligan—go see him together. Jenni, Whiskies and Archie Love. We'll give him the lot."

"Including Chick McAllister?"

Laidlaw considered for a moment. "Maybe keep that to ourselves for the time being."

"Because you want to be the one to question him?"

"Are you asking to be put on the guest list?"

Lilley's mouth twitched. "Why did you ask about the flowers?"

"Cam Colvin removed them. No need for Jenni to know that, but it tells me something."

"He knew about the pair of them?"

"Probably guessed that's who they'd be from."

Lilley nodded his understanding, then reached into the side pocket of the driver's door. The sheet of paper he held up listed the addresses they were supposed to be doorstepping. Laidlaw took it from him and pretended to peruse it for a moment, before ripping it in half and tossing it onto the back seat.

"Let's go see if what we're about to tell Milligan gets us a Cub Scout badge."

"Hard to imagine you in the Cubs, Jack."

"Boys' Brigade all the way, Bob. We used to shit on the Cubs from a great height."

"Metaphorically, I hope."

"Ask no questions and I'll tell you no lies. Any chance of you getting this jalopy started? Red carpet waiting for us at Central Division when we bring them the news."

14

They felt it as soon as they stepped inside the police station. It was as if an electric current had been run into the building. Everyone seemed to be in movement, and those movements became more frantic the nearer Laidlaw and Lilley got to the crime squad office. Laidlaw was eventually able to stop one detective constable in his tracks by dint of planting his feet directly in front of him, blocking any escape.

"What's going on?" he asked.

"A knife's been found. DI Milligan reckons it'll be the murder weapon."

"Found where?"

"A kid was waving it around in a park. Don't ask me which one."

"Why not? Aren't you supposed to be CID?"

The young officer's neck began to redden. He squeezed past Laidlaw and strode towards his destination.

Lilley was in the office by the time Laidlaw caught up. Every available telephone was turning hot in the grip of the shirtsleeved detectives. The room was stifling. Milligan stood beside his murder wall, barking orders. He wanted a fingertip search of the area.

"Grab as many uniforms as you need. This takes priority. And get me a map of Springburn Park!"

Springburn Park meant Balornock, not far from Stobhill Hospital. Laidlaw could visualise the old clock tower that greeted you as you drove towards the main building. He seemed to remember that the park wasn't big but boasted a bowling green, bandstand and maybe a football pitch. He was almost in Milligan's flushed face before the man recognised him.

"Change of plan. You'll be doorstepping in Springburn and Balornock."

"Are you sure it's our knife?"

"Kid says he found it hidden in bushes. He was waving it around so we got a call. The officer who caught up with him noticed some blood on the hilt."

"A bloodied knife dumped in Glasgow? Probably only happens a dozen times a day."

Milligan glowered at him. "If you engaged your brain as often as your mouth, you'd know there've only been three stabbings since Bobby Carter, and each time we caught the culprit and seized the weapon." He paused for a breath that was probably intended to be calming. "Somebody's drawing up an initial list of streets we need to visit. And by 'we,' I mean you."

"I couldn't be more thrilled. Has the knife gone to the lab?"

"Screws are being turned as we speak—I want a match by the end of today."

"The kid's prints will need to be eliminated."

Milligan nodded distractedly. "Where's that map?" he called out to the room at large.

"Donald's off to buy one," a voice replied. Laidlaw moved so that he was back in Milligan's eyeline.

"Can I help you?" Milligan enquired.

"Is the kid giving a statement?"

Milligan nodded again, then moved past Laidlaw in search of fresh prey.

Lilley was standing by his desk, holding up the revised list of addresses. Laidlaw replied with an approximation of a frown and walked out of the office, heading for the station's two interview rooms. The boy was in one of them, seated next to a woman who could have been a relative or some sort of social worker. The detective across the table stopped writing on his pad at Laidlaw's arrival.

"Tell me what you've told everyone else," Laidlaw said to the boy. He was ten or eleven, clear-eyed but scruffy. He'd probably already given up on school, preferring to take his lessons from the street.

"Found it in the bushes. I was just playing with it. I didn't mean anything." His tone strived for a studied indifference his twitching limbs could not match.

"And you didn't see anyone toss it?" Laidlaw watched the boy shake his head. "Was it well hidden or easy to spot?"

"It was just lying there on the dirt, between the grass and the bushes."

"As long as it's the only thing that was lying, you'll be fine."

He made his exit and stood in the corridor, arms folded. Several days now since the murder. If the knife used had been lying in plain view all that time, somebody would have found it prior to the kid. It had either been dislodged from a deeper hiding place or else it had been ditched more recently. If the latter, why? Had something spooked the killer? A sense of the net closing in? Had their conscience maybe played a role, the knife a continually gnawing reminder that they had committed an atrocity? In which case, Laidlaw and his colleagues were dealing not with a cold-blooded assassin but someone working at a deeper emotional level. Then again, why not ensure the knife was never found? The Clyde would have been a safer bet, or a rubbish bin somewhere. Yet bushes had been chosen rather than even the shallowest grave. That spoke of panic. And a panicked killer was easier to identify than one who remained cool-headed.

He heard a sneeze coming from behind a nearby door. Not the interview room the boy was in but the one next to it. He knocked and entered. A man in his mid twenties sat there alone. He was smoking his third or fourth cigarette and had scrunched up an empty plastic cup. He had lank hair and wore a black leather jacket beneath a faded denim waistcoat. Boots with steel toecaps and flared denims with the bottom three inches turned up.

"Who are you?" he asked Laidlaw.

"DC Laidlaw. Everything all right here?"

"That bastard Milligan's forgotten about me. Five more minutes and I'm walking."

"You must be Malky Chisholm." When the man made no denial, Laidlaw drew out the chair across from him and sat down, lighting a cigarette for himself. "How's business?"

"What business?"

"The gang business. Given any football hooligans a kicking lately? Scared any shopkeepers? How about graffiti—bit of spray-painting on the back wall of the Parlour?"

"Don't know what you're talking about."

"I'm talking about the forthcoming war and wondering which side you'll be taking."

"Who says a war's coming?"

"It is, though. One of Colvin's crew—and not just any old lackey, but a key player—executed and left on display on John Rhodes's turf. It's eye-for-an-eye stuff."

"So pull in John Rhodes."

"We need to know who put your team's name on that wall. If it was one of you, and it dates back to before Bobby Carter drew his last agonised breath, we can let it rest. On the other hand, if you can swear that none of your lot put it there, that means maybe someone's looking to maximise the potential mischief by adding you to the lengthening list of suspects."

"Any chance of getting that in English?"

Laidlaw gave a sigh that was only ninety per cent theatre. "That graffiti's got DI Milligan thinking you might be involved.

Could be that's exactly what the killer wants. If Cam Colvin starts seeing it that way, too, he'll come after you. Only course of action open to you then will be to go running to John Rhodes for protection."

Chisholm considered this for the best part of a minute while he finished his cigarette.

"It was probably one of my lot," he admitted. "I only heard about it after. Bit cheeky to plant it there, being Toi territory, but that was the whole point."

"Like staking your flag in the enemy camp?" Laidlaw nodded his understanding. "And how long ago was this?"

"Weeks. Maybe months, even. So can I go now? I've wasted half the day already."

"Answer me this first—who do you think killed Bobby Carter?"

"Someone sending a message to his boss." Chisholm shrugged at the obviousness of the answer.

"Who, though?"

"Got to be John Rhodes, hasn't it?" Chisholm was getting to his feet.

"Where do you think you're going?"

"You said we were done."

"Maybe you and me, but you're here until Milligan says otherwise."

"How long's that going to take?"

"The longer the better, as far as the law-abiding folk of your patch are concerned."

Chisholm slumped back onto his chair. "Ever hear the saying, all coppers are bastards?"

Laidlaw paused with the door ajar. "At least I'm a bastard with a glimmer of self-awareness." He flicked the remains of his cigarette towards the table and made his exit.

15

S pringburn Park was a sea of uniforms, their slow, linear progress watched by about half the local populace. Most of the doors knocked on, there'd been nobody home. They were either at work or the shops, or else they were gathered by the park railings to witness the spectacle.

"Here's hoping Cam Colvin appreciates the lengths we're going to," Laidlaw said to Bob Lilley.

"You don't sound hopeful."

"That's because I'm not. Even if it turns out to be the knife, what is all this telling us?"

"It's by the book, Jack."

"Aye, but the book's in a foreign language and missing some pages. Do you think the killer lives locally?"

"It's not all church ministers and spinster librarians around here."

"You're probably right, and if the killer hung on to the knife that means they'll have bloodstains on their clothes." Laidlaw gestured towards the crowd of onlookers. "Maybe you should walk up and down the line looking for telltale signs."

"Except the clothes will have been tossed by now. Same goes for any bag they might have kept the knife in."

"They didn't leave the knife with the body—that's something to think about. And this place is too public to be the scene of the crime. So now we have three distinct geographical locations to keep us busy—this park, the lane behind the Parlour, and wherever the stabbing actually took place. It's a few miles from here to the Calton. My guess would be that the third point of the triangle isn't too near either of those."

"They're covering their tracks, in other words?"

"Either that or they're monumentally stupid. Speaking of which . . ." Laidlaw was watching over Lilley's shoulder as Milligan came bounding towards them in a cream-coloured terylene raincoat, its belt flapping. His face was more flushed even than usual.

"One of the houses we tried, the wife was home but not the husband. Her name's Mary Thomson and she wasn't exactly cooperative. Officer asked at a neighbour's, and guess who she's married to—only Spanner Thomson."

"Isn't he one of Colvin's men?" Lilley checked.

"Bingo," Milligan said.

"We've some news of our own," Laidlaw broke in. "Carter was seeing a young lassie called Jennifer Love. She's the daughter of Archie Love."

Milligan's face creased in concentration. "The footballer?"

"Though as far as we know, her father had no idea they were an item," Lilley added.

Laidlaw could see Milligan struggling to accept this new strand. He already had a pattern in mind and didn't want it spoiled. He flapped a hand in front of him. "That's for later," he decided. "For now, I want Spanner Thomson brought in."

"Interview rooms are already taken," Laidlaw reminded him.

"The lad's gone home."

"And Malky Chisholm?"

"Can stew until I'm good and ready. Are you two okay to pick up Thomson?"

"Is he likely to have his trademark about his person?" Lilley enquired.

"I'm pretty sure that's why we're being given the job," Laidlaw answered.

"Just be careful, Bob," Milligan said. "DC Laidlaw's usual ploy of talking the suspect into submission might not work where a pipe wrench is involved. I'll see you back at the station. Either that or your hospital bed. Don't expect grapes." He moved off again, readying to inspect his troops.

"Except maybe sour ones," Laidlaw muttered.

"I suppose we could try asking the wife where we might find him," Lilley said without enthusiasm.

"Or we could just barge into any number of Cam Colvin's establishments while making a nuisance of ourselves. You got any idea what he looks like?"

"Not much hair, squat and chunky, high-pitched voice."

"I think I know him. He had a handful of the landlord's shirt front when I dropped into the Parlour. If I'd arrived a minute or two later, the pipe wrench might have been getting some air."

Lilley puffed out his cheeks and exhaled. "It's actually a spanner, hence the nickname. I'm not sure DI Milligan knows there's a difference. Where should we start, do you think?"

"This time of day, maybe the cab office."

"The cab office it is," Bob Lilley agreed.

16

N o one at the cab office, however, had ever heard of anyone called Spanner Thomson or Cam Colvin, cross their heart and hope to die, so Laidlaw and Lilley jumped back in the car and tried two separate bookies' shops, where again ignorance was akin to bliss. As they left the second, however, instinct told Laidlaw that maybe they should sit in the car for a minute. Sure enough, a youth soon left the betting shop and crossed the road, disappearing inside a drinking club. The detectives followed him and found Cam Colvin and his men in the main room, parked around a circular table, their card game having just been interrupted by the messenger. The air was thick with smoke. Open bottles of spirits were dotted around the table, along with piles of coins and notes.

"I'm guessing the house always wins," Laidlaw said, hands in pockets, feet spread as he faced Cam Colvin.

"Do I know you?"

"Your sidekicks do. I'm DC Laidlaw."

"I've heard the name, but that's about all."

"Nice to see you again, lads." Laidlaw turned back towards Colvin, who was doing his best not to let his puzzlement show. "They didn't tell you that I chased them out of the Parlour?"

"You're lucky you were still standing when we walked out of there," one of the men snarled. Laidlaw kept his attention on Colvin.

"See," he said, "that right there could be construed as a threat towards an officer of the law. Sort of thing that could lead to court proceedings for all concerned. Lucky for you we're here on other business. It concerns Mr. Thomson." He nodded towards the man with the smallest amount of money in front of him. "Looks like we'll be doing him a favour, too. One more bad hand would wipe him out."

"What's going on?" Thomson asked in his almost falsetto voice.

"Murder weapon found in the park near your home," Laidlaw informed him.

"Which murder is that, then?" Colvin asked.

"Your right-hand man, Bobby Carter."

"Nothing to do with me!" Thomson barked. The eyes of the other gang members were on him.

"Shouldn't take long at the station, then," Lilley said affably. "And like DC Laidlaw says, we'll be saving you from possible financial ruin and the wrath of your good lady wife."

Laidlaw had noted Thomson's hand edging towards the jacket that was draped over the back of his chair. "Don't do anything stupid," he said. "Your boss wouldn't like what happens next."

"I'm not sure I'm liking any of this," Colvin said quietly. "But the man's right, Spanner. Best if you go with them and answer their questions."

Thomson threw him a pleading look, in the hope of persuading him of his innocence. In return, Colvin gave a little nod, bottom lip pushed out slightly. Thomson rose slowly to his feet and lifted his jacket from the chair.

"Can't have you carrying a weapon," Lilley advised. There was another nod from Colvin, so Thomson took the spanner from its specially sewn pocket and placed it on the table, where it gleamed against the green baize. He then scooped up what little money sat next to it.

"If you're minded to get rough with him," Colvin told the detectives, "you'll be paid back tenfold, that's a promise." He paused. "You must see what's happening here. Kill one of my men and then try sticking another in the frame. It's so obvious it's almost insulting."

"We *will* find whoever did it, trust me on that," Laidlaw said. "It'd be nice to get on with that job without the Battle of the Bulge erupting all around us."

Colvin made show of checking his surroundings. "I don't see a battle—do any of you lads see one?"

There were shakes of the head.

"That's the thing about hostilities, though," Laidlaw said. "They creep towards you almost invisibly. You'll sense their approach but they can still surprise you, by which time it's too late. I'm guessing this card game is a regular thing, so it had to happen, otherwise you might look overly rattled by events and that would get back to the likes of John Rhodes and Matt Mason. Doesn't pay to let weakness show, whether you're playing cards or doing business."

Colvin seemed to be trying to take the measure of Laidlaw. He even leaned back a little in his chair as if this might help. But in the end all he did was shake his head at the impossibility of the task.

"Don't keep him out too late," he said, turning back to the hand of cards in front of him. "Whose turn was it to bet?"

"I've not done nothing," Thomson felt it necessary to stress as he followed Bob Lilley towards the door. "I tell you, I've not."

"And we believe you when you say that," Laidlaw assured him. "We accept that statement one hundred per cent."

He couldn't resist a final backwards glance towards the table. Colvin was picking up a card from the deck, placing it in his hand and discarding another. The spanner had become mere ornamentation. The game progressed almost as if the existence of the police inquiry had no meaning here.

As soon as the door was closed, however, Colvin tossed his cards onto the table. He was vibrating with rage.

"If any of you knows anything, this is definitely the time to speak."

Mickey Ballater, Dod Menzies and Panda Paterson shared looks and shrugs. Paterson cleared his throat.

"You know what Bobby was like. We all had words with him from time to time."

"Just words, though," Menzies said, as though he were underlining a sentence in a primary-school jotter.

"Teasing mostly," Ballater agreed. "Which isn't to say Bobby didn't sometimes deserve more."

"You mean a punch? A slap? A doing?" Colvin's eyes had narrowed even further than usual.

"I just mean he sometimes got a bit up himself. He'd have a drink in him from some club or other and maybe some dolly bird in tow who he was trying to impress and he'd start winding us up, telling everyone we were his message boys and he was the grocer."

"We're not going to speak ill of the dead," Paterson added, "and nobody around this table harmed a hair on his head— God's honest truth—but the guy could be hard work, and I think that got to Spanner more than the rest of us."

"Oh aye?"

Paterson was looking for someone to back him up, but his friends seemed suddenly to have been deprived of the power of speech.

"You've known Spanner longer than any of us," he explained to Colvin, "and that's important to him. You're like a brother or something. Then Bobby arrives and things start to change. You're not confiding in Spanner the way you used to. Now it's late-night drinks with just you and Bobby."

"Bobby understood the business in a way Spanner never could." Colvin was beginning to look slightly uncomfortable.

"That's what it comes down to and that's all those drinks were ever about."

Paterson nodded his agreement. "I'm just saying, Spanner would go to the scaffold for you."

"Lucky we've done away with hanging then, eh?" Because Colvin was attempting to lighten the mood, there were wary chuckles at this. "I take your point, though, and it begs a question—did anyone give Spanner cause to feel that Bobby might need more than a talking-to? Maybe that he was dipping his hand in the till or playing a bit naughty?" Colvin watched each man shake his head. Only Panda Paterson dared to make eye contact as he did so. "Because I did hear a rumour," Colvin continued, his words slowing almost to a crawl, "that Matt Mason was saying he had someone inside my shop whispering sweet nothings in his ear. I know what Mason's like so I dismissed it as his usual bullshit, but now I'm starting to wonder."

"You're sure it was Mason?" Dod Menzies piped up.

"Why?" The question came like a bullet.

"It's just I'd have thought that's the sort of sleekit tactic John Rhodes would use—get us all watching each other, not sure who to trust."

"You're maybe right, so let me turn things on their head. Say Bobby not only heard those rumours but went and did a bit of investigating."

Panda Paterson was shaking his head. "This isn't doing us any good, boss. We all know the obvious candidates—John Rhodes and Matt Mason. But Mason's been in hospital getting his leg seen to and he seems happy enough with the territory he owns. Rhodes is another matter entirely. He's the one we should be putting the screws on. If he's innocent, only way to get us off his back is to help us find whoever did do it. We make life difficult for him until he does right by us."

"You're saying I can trust you—all of you, Spanner included?"

"I'm saying you have to, or everything we've built falls apart."

"Trust's a two-way street, though—how come you didn't tell me about meeting Laidlaw at the Parlour?"

"He sort of did send us packing," Dod Menzies said. "That's why we kept our traps shut. You might say our professional pride took a dent."

"It's your heads that'll be taking a dent if you keep anything else back from me, understood?"

"Yes, boss."

Colvin had picked up his cards again without really looking at them. He tossed them onto the pile of discards. "Let's start a new game then. Increase the stakes, take a few risks. Is everybody in?"

All three men agreed that they were.

17

The two women walked through the Necropolis at a pace that was stately, befitting their surroundings and purpose. Eleanor Love always brought them on a slightly circuitous route so that they would pass the statue of John Knox. As he frowned his disapproval down on them, so Eleanor Love scowled back. Despite the reason for their visit, this always made Jennifer Love smile. For the past several years she had been tasked with carrying the small posy of flowers. The grave itself was neat and tidy; her mother made sure of that on her regular visits. But today was Sam's birthday and Jennifer always accompanied her, as she did, too, when commemorating the day Sam had died.

The name Sam had been Archie Love's choice. *My son Sam, Samson, you see?* He had hoped to watch Sam become big and strong, had had the laddie kicking a ball almost before he could balance unaided on his plump and wobbly infant legs. Dead by the age of eight, two years older than Jennifer, who had taken some persuading that her big brother wouldn't be coming back from playing in the courtyard behind his best pal's tenement.

They had reached the graveside now, Jennifer handing over the flowers, her mother crouching to place them in the small vase, grown opaque from weathering. No words were spoken, and afterwards, as was now traditional, the two women stood in contemplation of their surroundings. The Necropolis was where the city's great and good finally rubbed stone shoulders with everybody else. Eleanor Love reached out and gave her daughter's hand a brief but tight squeeze.

"Why does Dad never come?" Jennifer asked. It was far from the first time the question had passed her lips.

Eleanor gave a slow exhalation. "He's not a bad man, your dad. This here is why he's always wanted what's best for you."

"Sam fell off a wall, Mum. I don't need wrapped in cotton wool because of that."

"I know. But look at the trouble you . . ." She broke off, swallowing the rest of the sentence.

"I'm not in trouble. I've never *been* in trouble. But everybody surely merits a bit of freedom."

"Your dad just wants—"

"What's best for me. So you keep saying. But does he ever wonder what I want?" Jennifer dug a toe into the damp grass in front of her.

"Your good shoes," her mother reminded her.

"Why do we always end up talking about him anyway? I don't mean Sam, I mean Dad. Maybe one day we'll talk about us. Maybe we'll talk about *you*."

"What about me?"

"Anything. Everything. What were you like when you were my age? What did you want from life?"

Eleanor Love thought for a moment. "I was already pregnant," she said, her eyes on the headstone. Jennifer watched as those eyes began to fill with tears.

"I'm sorry, Mum," she said, reaching into her bag for a paper handkerchief. But as she made to dab at her mother's face, Eleanor's hand clasped itself around her wrist.

"Swear you don't know anything, Jenni. Here in front of Sam. Promise me you don't know what happened to him."

"You mean Bobby?" Jennifer shook her head, not quite meeting her mother's eyes. She could feel her fierce stare, though, as the hankie went to work. "Cross my heart," she said, her voice little more than a whisper.

And it was true, mostly. She didn't *know* anything, nothing that would stand up in court. But she had an inkling, maybe even more than an inkling.

"Ready for that cup of tea now?" she said. "The café's keeping us the table by the window."

Eleanor had released her grip on her daughter's wrist. She gave a slow nod.

"Has Dad said anything about Bobby?" Jennifer enquired, trying to sound casual. "Since the news broke, I mean?"

"He still doesn't know. Best if it's kept that way, wouldn't you say?"

"Thanks, Mum. I mean it." Jennifer gave her mother a hug, Eleanor closing her eyes the better to appreciate the warmth of it. Then Eleanor Love allowed herself to be led from the Necropolis, almost as if their roles had been reversed and she was now the child.

Laidlaw often thought of the Calton as "Little Rhodesia." It had the feel of a separate state, John Rhodes having declared UDI. The Gay Laddie belied its name by being another unwelcoming slab of 1950s architecture, its windows high up and ungenerous, its walls rough-plastered, ripe for graffiti yet unsullied by it. Laidlaw knew the reason why: this was John Rhodes's second home. To defile it would be to invite swift and definitive retribution. As he walked in, he was scrutinised by a line of drinkers at the bar who might as well have been wearing the uniforms of security guards. They saw him immediately for what he was, even though they couldn't be sure *who* he was. He ignored them and waited for the barman to grace him with some attention.

"I need a word with John," he explained, glancing in the direction of the snug.

"Is he expecting you?"

"We're not in an episode of *Upstairs Downstairs*, Charlie, and you'd make a shite Gordon Jackson. Go tell the man I'm here, and make sure to say I *need* a word rather than want one."

The barman put down the glass he'd been drying and flipped the tea towel over his left shoulder, then headed towards the snug. Laidlaw knew he was being studied like a medical specimen as he lit a cigarette. He kept his face to the row of quarter-gill optics behind the bar. There was no television, no music, and until he vacated the room there'd be no more conversation. The tension in the bar was probably at its usual level, these being men who treated every waking moment and passing stranger as a potential threat.

When Charlie the barman re-emerged, he reached beneath the counter and handed Laidlaw an unopened bottle of the good whisky and two glasses. "John doesn't take water," he said, meaning none would be offered for Laidlaw.

With the cigarette gripped between his teeth, Laidlaw walked into the snug. At one time its purpose would have been to protect women from the masculine world of the main bar. Now it held only John Rhodes and his bodyguard, the one with the face disfigured by razor scars. Rhodes tended to change bodyguards regularly, so that they didn't become soft and lazy. This one had been around longer than most, long enough in fact that it might be worth Laidlaw's time finding out his name. Not right now, though. After a nod in the man's direction, he placed the bottle and glasses on the table and seated himself opposite Rhodes. He knew better than to open the bottle. That was Rhodes's duty. An inch of amber duly appeared in Laidlaw's glass, half as much again in Rhodes's.

"I hear you've picked up Spanner Thomson," Rhodes said without preamble.

"News travels fast."

"It might make sense, I suppose—all businesses have their power struggles and fallings-out."

"Any reason to think Thomson had a particular falling-out with Bobby Carter?"

"Spanner and Colvin go back to schooldays. Carter arrived later."

"Simple jealousy, then."

Rhodes sipped his drink before meeting Laidlaw's eyes for the first time. "Carter wanted to see me. We arranged to meet at the Parlour. In the end, I didn't show up."

"Why not?"

"I wasn't sure it would end well."

"How long ago was this?"

"Three or four weeks back."

Laidlaw gave a slight nod. The timing chimed with the story Conn Feeney had given him.

"Any idea what he wanted?"

"Two theories—one, negotiating to switch sides, sounding out what sort of offer I might make."

"And the other?"

"Carter enjoyed the life. He didn't just set up camp in the picture house when *The Godfather* came out, he'd read the book a few times, too. Rumour was, he wanted his own slice of Glasgow. If I gave him a bit and Colvin gave him a bit, he'd create a kind of buffer zone between us, meaning less potential for strife."

"That would have been ambitious."

"Bobby Carter was an ambitious man. He knew he had a brain and he reckoned that made him better than most."

"Had he talked to Colvin, do you think?"

"No idea. But say someone like Spanner Thomson found out. You can see how that might have escalated."

"Or else Spanner took the info to his boss, who flipped, did Carter in himself, and popped the carcass on your doorstep to blur the picture." Laidlaw paused for a moment, deep in thought, then roused himself. "And speaking of escalations, how are things between you and Colvin right now?"

Rhodes's look hardened. "There are some questions you don't get to ask."

"And yet my job demands that I do. But I'm happy to change the subject to Chick McAllister."

"What's Chick got to do with anything?"

"I need a chat with him, that's all. I'm sure he'll fill you in afterwards."

"You don't ask much, do you?"

"Just as much as I need." Laidlaw lifted his glass and sipped.

"Does Milligan really expect Spanner Thomson to break down and confess?"

"He's one of life's eternal optimists."

"But you know better, don't you?"

"I try."

The two men sat in silence until Rhodes angled his head quarter of an inch in the direction of the scarred man, this being as much as was necessary.

"Go rustle up Chick."

After the man had left, Rhodes gave Laidlaw his full attention. "Are you wondering how he got the scars?"

"Asking too many questions?"

This almost elicited a smile. "I gave him them. This was a few years before he came to work for me."

"You trust him not to want payback?"

"Those *were* payback, meaning the books are balanced between us. Seems to me I'm the one doling out favours to you and it's all been a one-way street so far. If war does break out, I hope you'll remember that."

"There's nothing wrong with my memory."

"That's good to hear, because with Thomson in custody

Colvin is two men down and I foresee a lot of headless chickens running around."

"The sort of mayhem that could be capitalised on."

"You know yourself that these reckonings happen from time to time. It clears the air the way a thunderstorm does, and afterwards the boundaries are re-established, meaning everybody's happy."

"The ones still able to walk, talk and feed themselves without assistance," Laidlaw qualified.

The scarred man was back in the room again.

"He'll be here in five," he said.

Rhodes nodded and focused on Laidlaw again. "But he's not going to tell you a thing until I know what you need from him."

Laidlaw considered for a moment. "McAllister went out with a young woman called Jennifer Love. After they broke up, Carter took her under his wing."

"And you think that gives Chick a motive to do in Bobby Carter?"

"Not especially, but when I give the connection to Milligan, he might. All I'm doing here is trying to rule him out to my own satisfaction so the investigation doesn't waste any more time than it already has."

"In other words, you've not told your colleagues about Chick and Jennifer Love?" Rhodes pressed his palms against the surface of the table as if readying to commence a seance. Laidlaw knew that he was storing the information away. Here was a detective who didn't always take everything to his bosses, a detective capable of keeping secrets.

Maybe a rare cop John Rhodes could trust without money changing hands.

The gesture had revealed the large gold wristwatch on his left wrist. He seemed to notice the time and slowly rose to his feet.

"You stay here and ask Chick your questions. I've got business elsewhere."

"Don't do anything I wouldn't do, John."

Laidlaw was rewarded with another thin smile. The scarred man started to help Rhodes into his camel-hair coat.

"Any relation to the footballer?" Rhodes asked, almost too casually.

"Who are we talking about?"

"Archie Love. It's not the most common surname."

"He's her father, aye," Laidlaw conceded, watching Rhodes closely, wondering what was happening behind eyes that hadn't yet blinked. No more was said, however, as the two men departed the snug. Laidlaw rolled his shoulders and neck a few times to loosen the knots, Rhodes having turned him, too, into an actor for the duration, one learning his lines a split second before having to deliver them. He was getting out another cigarette when the barman appeared, placing a jug of water on the table.

"Mr. Rhodes thought you might take a splash," he explained.

"Mr. Rhodes is well informed, but I think I need a breather. It's like all the air's been sucked out of this place and replaced by testosterone."

"You're not waiting for Chick?"

"While every ear in the place listens in?" Laidlaw shook his head and polished off the dregs in his glass. The same row of faces stood at the bar as he made his exit. He blew each of them a kiss.

It wasn't quite raining outside, but dusk was falling, the headlights of cars and buses picking out pedestrians shuffling home from work or shopping. Their world was not his and they wouldn't thank him for sharing. He wondered if Glasgow would always be like this. Change had to come, surely. Jobs couldn't keep vanishing, the gangs becoming more feral, people's lives more fraught. But then a young mother trundled past pushing a pram, transfixed by it as if she had just invented the world's first baby. To her, Laidlaw didn't exist. To her, nothing mattered except the new life she was nurturing and nothing in the world was off kilter as long as that nurturing continued uninterrupted.

"Hope springs eternal," he found himself saying out loud. He remembered his old school pal Tom Docherty. They'd spent many a night as students quoting poetry and exchanging the names of cult authors, usually in the Admiral pub, usually between games of darts or cards or dominoes. But Laidlaw had quit his course after one year and he didn't know where Tom was. His brother Scott might know, but Laidlaw didn't really know his whereabouts either. Like Tom, Scott had dreamed of becoming a writer some day, either that or an artist. The last news Laidlaw had had was that he was teaching in their old home town of Graithnock. An address or phone number would be simple enough to find, but something had stopped him thus far. His feeling was, Scott hadn't made the effort so why should he? The old Scots word "thrawn" came to mind. The two brothers had always locked horns, maybe too similar to one another for their own good. It hadn't helped that Laidlaw had joined the police—switching sides, as Scott, always the first to the barricades, would have put it.

The taxi that drew to a halt in front of him seemed more of a private chauffeur service, no money changing hands as the passenger stepped out onto the pavement.

"Perks of the job?" Laidlaw asked conversationally, receiving a glower in response. "I'm the man you're here to see," he explained. "Always supposing you're Chick McAllister."

"We not going in?" McAllister enquired. He was tall, early twenties, with thick waves of hair falling over his ears and neck. The amount of denim he wore reminded Laidlaw that he should buy shares in Lee Cooper.

"This won't take long," Laidlaw informed him. "In fact, you should have told your driver to wait. All I'm wanting to ask is, did you stab Bobby Carter to death a few nights back?"

McAllister's mouth opened a fraction in disbelief. "You're joking, aren't you?"

"You knew he was seeing your old girlfriend."

"They'd already split up, though."

"And how did you feel about that?"

"Mr. Rhodes said I had to talk to you, but I'm thinking maybe that's a bad idea."

"What's your role in the organisation, Chick? You don't look like muscle and you've no visible war wounds, so I'm guessing supply side. A busy night at Whiskies must be the jackpot, eh? Is it just dope, or do you flog pills as well?"

"I'm not doing this." McAllister turned to go.

"Don't make me have to give you a bad report when I talk to John Rhodes."

McAllister pivoted to face him. "I never touched Bobby Carter. I hardly knew the guy."

"But you'd seen him around? At Whiskies? With Jenni?"

"I told her he was no good for her and for once she took my advice."

"Ever meet her dad?"

"She took me home once. Her mum was there but not her dad."

"Who else knew about Jenni and Carter?"

"Word has a way of getting around."

"Did Carter's boss know?"

"Definitely."

"Carter's wife?"

McAllister shrugged. "Bobby Carter spread himself a bit thin where women were concerned. That was one of the things I told Jenni."

"What else did you tell her?"

"That he was trouble."

"Trouble how?"

"He worked for Cam Colvin, didn't he?"

"And you work for John Rhodes. Two cheeks of the same arse, no?"

McAllister's face reddened with anger. Laidlaw watched and waited, but he could tell McAllister was not a violent man, unlike most of the drinkers the other side of the Gay Laddie's door. He was a drone, and Laidlaw was not in the market for drones.

"Nice talking to you," he said, crossing the road and heading to the nearest bus stop.

Laidlaw waited until it had just gone six before heading to Central Division, arriving at the crime squad office to find it deserted, only the warm fug indicating that bodies had inhabited its space until recently. Browsing the murder wall, he saw that an identikit photo had been added next to pictures of Springburn Park. A note indicated that the identikit matched a description of a man seen in the park just prior to the knife being found. Laidlaw couldn't help but give a humourless chuckle. In his experience—and here was further proof—such photos looked like everyone and no one. You could turn most of them upside down and they'd make as much sense. Instead, he focused for a moment on the photo of Monica Carter, remembering again the pathologist's words about Cam Colvin, and Colvin himself placing a hand on her elbow as she spoke to the reporters. Looking around, he saw a copy of that evening's paper dumped in a waste-paper bin and lifted it out. There she was on the front page, Colvin right next to her, their hips almost touching.

Crossing to his desk, he started sifting the piles of paperwork. He read the notes made by Milligan on first visiting the family home. The place was in the midst of renovation and redecoration and consequently fairly chaotic, but Milligan felt obliged to state that "normally it would be a welcoming and very pleasant environment," as if he were an estate agent pitching to sell the place. The three Carter children had been present in the living room along with their mother. Mrs. Carter was praised for her "surface calmness." The daughter, Stella, had offered the visitors tea. In "difficult circumstances" the family were "doing their level best" and their cooperation was "total and appreciated."

"Christ, Milligan," Laidlaw muttered to himself, "you're not writing Mills and Boon." He tossed the report to one side and started looking for information on Cam Colvin and his men. There was a whole folder's worth, detailing the usual litany of maimed and feral childhoods, broken homes and early transgressions that would come to be leveraged into criminal careers, any alternatives seemingly unobtainable. Spanner Thomson's father had been absent throughout his childhood and his mother had been too fond of the bottle and one-night stands. Truancy, shoplifting and borstal eventually became the youngster's CV, followed by gang affiliation and a position of trust in his friend Cam Colvin's outfit. Colvin himself was slightly different. He was following in the family business, both his father and paternal grandfather having spent more of their adulthood inside prisons than outside of them. Then there was the incident involving the blade embedded between his shoulder blades, which had proved no mean calling card.

The autobiographies of Panda Paterson, Dod Menzies and Mickey Ballater were not dissimilar, except insofar as Ballater had achieved decent grades at school and stuck it out, leaving for a job in manufacturing until lured by the easier money presented by gangland life. He'd been questioned by police many times but never formally charged, putting him on a par with Cam Colvin himself, the other members of the gang having served a variety of short sentences during their careers. An occupational hazard, they would doubtless call it.

It was only when a cleaner arrived to empty the bins that Laidlaw looked up from his reading. Checking his watch, he saw that a couple of hours had passed. He stretched his spine and rolled his shoulders.

"Kept behind as a punishment?" the cleaner asked as she pushed a sweeping brush across the floor.

"Headmaster's a sod," Laidlaw informed her.

"Picking on you, eh? And you as pure as the driven snow."

"That's me all right."

He got up from his desk, deciding he'd had enough bleakness for one day. He hoped it was still raining outside. He felt the need of a cleansing shower.

"That you done, son? If you don't mind me saying, you look dead beat. Are you sure he's worth it?"

"Everybody counts," Laidlaw said, heading for the door.

18

When he got to the Burleigh, Jan handed him a message. It was from Bob Lilley and included Lilley's home number.

"There's a phone down the hall," Jan said. Laidlaw dug into his pocket, bringing out a meagre selection of coins, and she relented. "Okay, use the one in the office—just don't go telling the management."

With a smile of thanks he followed her past the desk and into the cramped room behind. She brushed past him as she left. He settled into her chair and dialled the number. A woman answered, presumably Margaret.

"Is Bob around? It's Jack Laidlaw."

"Oh, Jack. I was just talking about you. I spoke to Ena this afternoon. Nice of you to invite us for a bite."

Laidlaw's brow furrowed. "We don't often entertain," he eventually commented.

"Anyway, here's Bob."

Laidlaw listened as the handset was swapped over. A television or radio was on in the background. He envisaged a comfortable living room. His and hers chairs. Maybe a coffee table between them with the evening paper folded on it and coasters for the mugs.

"Hiya," Bob Lilley said.

"A bite to eat, Bob?"

"Hang on a sec. Margaret, any chance of a tea?" There were muffled sounds for a few moments. "That's her gone to the kitchen," Lilley explained. "Ena phoned Margaret. Got our number from the directory. They cooked this up between them, nothing to do with me."

"When is this delightful dinner party supposed to happen?"

"Tomorrow. Seven sharp."

Laidlaw expelled some air. There was a large canvas shoulder bag on the floor next to him, presumably Jan's. He began exploring the contents while the conversation continued. Make-up, keys, purse, an Agatha Christie paperback, a Mars bar and a packet of cheese and onion crisps, plus a scarf and fold-up umbrella. Her raincoat was on a peg behind the door.

"What's it in aid of, Bob?" he asked as he rummaged.

"I just think they got on well when they nattered. Now you and me are working together, they reckon this is the next obvious step."

"I'm not a great one for socialising."

"Pubs being the exception."

"That's work, though, mostly."

"You want me to try to postpone it? We can always say the case is keeping us too busy."

"Ena would see through that. Best to just let her have her way. So what's so urgent it couldn't wait till morning?"

"The dinner party's really the reason. Thought you'd want as much notice as possible."

"Any news from St. Andrews Street?"

"You'd know if you dropped in occasionally."

"I was just there, for your information, pulling an extra shift."

"You disappeared sharpish after we'd delivered Spanner Thomson, though."

"I had stuff to do."

"Feel like sharing the fruits?"

"Not quite yet. I don't suppose our resident genius Ernie Milligan managed to conjure a confession from Thomson?"

"We had to release him. He got a lawyer sharpish and that was that."

"And the knife?"

"Only dabs belong to the kid who found it. Blood type matches the victim, but that's as far as the lab are willing to go."

"The killer wiped his prints," Laidlaw stated.

"Or wore gloves. Either way, we're still treating it as the murder weapon, which means more door-to-door on the welcoming streets of Balornock."

"What about Malky Chisholm?"

"Milligan decided he'd had enough fun with him and let him go."

"One step forward, two steps back. We're in danger of drowning in details."

"Like we did with Bible John? Nights I spent at the Barrowland hoping he'd show his face . . ." Only three years had passed since the killer known as Bible John had taken his last known victim. He'd met all three at the Barrowland Ballroom, which was why undercover officers had swamped the place, to no avail.

"I bet you're a good dancer, though," Laidlaw commented.

"Problem was, so was the WPC I was partnered with. Caused a bit of friction with Margaret."

Laidlaw had turned his attention from Jan's bag to the items covering every inch of the desk. Paperwork, stapler, paper clips turned into a daisy chain, plus a Blackpool mug filled with pens and pencils, and a framed photo of two young kids. He picked the photo up and studied it. Taken on a summer beach, maybe even Blackpool itself.

"Will I see you for the briefing tomorrow?" Lilley was asking.

"Wouldn't miss it for the world. Does Margaret know about the Burleigh?"

"I've not told her."

"Ena probably will, if she hasn't already. I'm sorry you're being dragged into this."

"Into what?"

"Becoming pieces on the chessboard of my marriage."

"Can we bring anything?"

"Just yourselves, and maybe a couple of flak jackets."

Laidlaw ended the call and folded the note into his wallet. Could be he'd find Lilley's number useful in future. Jan had to squeeze herself against the reception desk so he could get past her.

"Nice picture," he said, gesturing towards the office.

"My niece and nephew."

"No kids of your own, then?"

"No encumbrances of any kind, Jack."

"Lucky you," he said as she handed him the key to his room.

"So, you know, if you ever wanted to invite me to a Lena Martell show . . ."

"Certainly beats the Black and White Minstrels."

"I've left you in the suite for another night. Is that all right with you?"

"It's a bit spacious for one person."

"Maybe you'll have to do something about that."

"Maybe I will," Laidlaw said with a faltering smile.

Two of them in the stolen car, the sleeping city unaware of their progress through its deserted streets. They kept their eyes on the road ahead, occasional glances to left and right as they passed a junction. You never knew. None of the police boxes showed a light on inside. There were hotel kitchens where the night beat often took refuge, keeping warm with refills from the kettle. Bakeries, too, where rolls fresh from the oven could be chewed. Why bother pounding the pavements when all the drunks had long gone home?

The bottles clinked, one against the other, nestling on the floor between the passenger's feet. His jaw was tight, his gloved fists tensed.

"This is us," his companion said, the first words to be spoken in a good five or ten minutes.

"Aye."

"I'll drive past, just to make sure."

"I know you will."

No lights in any of the nearby windows; no signs of life anywhere. So the driver executed a three-point turn and made the approach again, this time pulling to a stop kerbside.

"Right then," he said unnecessarily, since the passenger was already pushing open the door, reaching down to pick up both bottles. Then he was gone. The driver rolled down his window, realising he should have thought of that before. The smell of petrol was going to linger. Not that it mattered. The car's next destination would also be its final stop.

Scrapyard. Compactor. Gone.

The sky was turning orange as the two men drove away.

DAY FOUR

19

The message next morning said to forget the briefing and rendezvous at the Gay Laddie. As Laidlaw approached on foot, he could smell charred wood and blistered paint. Bob Lilley was eating a buttered roll. He held out a paper bag.

"Got you one," he said.

"Thanks." Laidlaw took a bite and started chewing as he surveyed the damage. There wasn't too much of it. The Gay Laddie was built like an atomic bunker. Its small windows were blackened, as was the area around the door.

"Thing about that door," Lilley mused, "looks like wood but it's actually steel. Not the sort of thing you can buy off the peg."

"And not cheap, either," Laidlaw agreed. "But worth it to somebody."

"That somebody being John Rhodes, I'd presume."

"Has he been for a look-see?"

"Not that I've heard."

Laidlaw approached the door. Shards of glass lay at his feet. The neck of the bottle was almost intact, strands of rag sticking to it.

"Taking a leaf out of Ulster's book," Lilley commented. "Two of Rhodes's men got hit, too. One answered a knock at his door, only to be met by a sledgehammer. The other was jumped walking home from a party."

"Makes sense. Colvin's a man down with another under

suspicion. Means he looks weak to the opposition, like a wounded animal. He's lashing out to try to slow them from coming for him."

"You reckon?"

Laidlaw took another bite of roll, wiping the dusting of flour from around his mouth. "Need tea or something to wash this down." There was a café across the street at the corner, so he headed there, Lilley a few steps behind. The tea was poured from an oversized, much-dented pewter pot, milk already added. A sugar bowl sat on the counter along with a used spoon. The place smelled of bacon fat, its cramped booths filled with people licking their wounds as they recovered from the night before. Laidlaw and Lilley stood at the counter as they drank.

"Not so much a city as a hangover," Laidlaw commented quietly. "One nobody can remember ordering. The fun beforehand, that's fine and dandy, but the consequences are always a shock to the system, and Glasgow's all consequences, every day of the week."

"It's a bit early for me, but don't let that stop you nipping my head. Margaret says, can we bring flowers for Ena—would she like that?"

"Don't ask me."

"Or chocolates maybe?"

"Bring a bottle of wine, any colour, any price. We've probably got a corkscrew." Laidlaw had disposed of the last remnants of roll and was brushing his fingers clean. "This tea's putting hairs on my tongue," he complained. "Is doorstepping around Springburn Park really all the day has to offer?"

"Milligan's already got people talking to Rhodes's walking wounded."

"It's Rhodes himself he should be having a word with. The man's duty-bound to retaliate, otherwise *he's* the one who looks weak—weak or else guilty."

"You're pretty sure he wasn't behind Carter's death, though?"

"Doesn't mean he'll deny it to anyone who asks."

"Because some will see it as a gallus move?" Lilley nodded his agreement with Laidlaw's assessment. "He didn't sanction it, but the fact it's happened doesn't exactly harm his reputation."

"I saw him again yesterday, by the way."

"Rhodes?"

"Right there in the Gay Laddie. He gave me Chick McAllister, but McAllister didn't have much to offer."

"So now can we mention McAllister to Ernie Milligan?"

"That's up to you, Bob."

"Playing down your role?"

"To a bare minimum, if that." Laidlaw lit a cigarette.

"Are you thinking of paying Rhodes another visit?"

"Rhodes isn't the one setting off firebombs."

"Cam Colvin, then?"

Laidlaw took in a lungful of smoke and offered a shrug. "This case is like one of those charm bracelets," he said as he exhaled. "New charms keep being added. They all mean something individually, even if they never quite meet on the bracelet itself."

"Is that how you're going to talk tonight? It's just that Margaret is more about knitting patterns, *Woman's Realm* and Sacha Distel."

Laidlaw thought for a moment. "Maybe bring *two* bottles of wine," he said.

20

Spanner Thomson locked the front door after him—two mortises as well as the Yale—and, as was his habit, looked to right and left as he walked down the narrow garden path. His car, an Austin Maxi, was parked at the kerb. He unlocked it and got in. When he turned the first corner, heading towards Springburn Road, a white Jaguar XJ6 pulled into the middle of the street, blocking the route. Thomson tensed, hands tightening on the steering wheel. The Jag's rear door had opened, a figure emerging. John Rhodes walked towards the Maxi, yanked open the passenger-side door and got in.

"This thing's more skip than car," he complained, kicking aside some of the debris in the footwell.

"I'd have had it hoovered if I'd known."

The Jaguar had pulled in close to the pavement again. Rhodes pointed to the cleared roadway. "Don't mind a bit of company, do you, Spanner? You can drop me long before you get to wherever you're going. Colvin still holding his war councils at the Coronach? I hear the owner's not happy that the tab never seems to get cleared."

"It wasn't me, Mr. Rhodes," Thomson said, his voice betraying only the slightest tremor as he pressed down on the accelerator. At the main road, he signalled to turn, something he seldom did. A pedestrian might have taken him for a pupil on his first driving lesson, even if the bulky figure filling the adjacent front seat looked nothing like an instructor.

"What wasn't you, Spanner?" John Rhodes asked.

"The Gay Laddie. That and your two boys."

"Grown men rather than boys. They should know how to defend themselves." Rhodes twisted his body to face Thomson. "But you've just told me that you do know about it, know it happened, I mean, and there's been nothing in the papers or on the radio as yet."

"Bush telegraph, Mr. Rhodes."

"You don't even have a phone in your house, Spanner. A neighbour takes messages for you and her laddie passes them on. You slip her a few quid a week for services rendered. That tells me you're not only cautious but you've got your wits about you, too."

Thomson checked in his rear-view mirror. The Jaguar was right behind him.

"Is there a message you want me to give to Mr. Colvin?"

"He'll be hearing from me, but not through you. I'm here because Milligan pulled you in."

"A fishing expedition, that's all."

"Conducted by a man who couldn't catch crabs in a knocking shop. You think the knife was planted near your house on purpose?"

"How do you mean?"

"To put you in the frame."

"No idea." Another signal, another manoeuvre. "What if it was?"

"Well, I'd maybe be curious as to who did it. It would have to be somebody who knows you live locally, somebody who either wants you out of the way or wants your boss relegating you to the subs' bench."

"You seem to have done a lot of thinking on the subject."

"The body was dumped on my patch, Spanner. I'm taking that as a very personal insult. And while I loathe your boss with every fibre of my being, I don't see how a war helps either of us. If someone's cornering us, I want to know who and why. Then again, it could be a falling-out amongst thieves, couldn't it? That's almost the simplest explanation. How far do you trust the likes of Panda Paterson, Mickey Ballater and Dod Menzies? With Carter gone, there are only four runners and riders in the race. One of you is going to end up in the winners' enclosure, and you've known Colvin longer than anyone. Maybe that makes you the favourite, and every betting man knows the favourite's the one most likely to get nobbled."

"I see what you're saying."

"I know you do, but you're also thinking it's what you'd expect me to say if I wanted to start taking Colvin and his organisation apart brick by brick."

"You'd want to sow dissent."

"Education wasn't lost on you, was it, Spanner? But the dissent's already there. Lobbing petrol at the Gay Laddie is amateur hour, which makes me think it wasn't Colvin's idea, meaning one of your colleagues was acting on his own initiative. That might be the very person you've got to watch out for." Thomson could feel John Rhodes's eyes drilling into him. "Time may come when you need a friend."

"And you're offering to be that friend?"

"Unless you want me as an enemy?" The look Rhodes was giving him had hardened still further. "Do you need telling that mercy's not high on my list of personal qualities? I learned long ago that there's no point being reasonable in an unreasonable world. This is the only time you and me will talk like this. And when I come for your boss—and I *will* come for him one of these days—if you're standing in my way I won't think twice, understood?"

"Understood."

Rhodes turned his attention from driver to windscreen, leaving a few moments of distilled silence before speaking again. He sniffed and gave a twitch of the mouth. "One last thing you need to know—Carter was planning to set up a rival outfit." He saw the look Thomson was giving him. "I know this counts as something else I'd say to stir up trouble. Doesn't mean it isn't true." He paused again. "Maybe your boss knew and maybe he didn't. If he *did* know, maybe he did something about it. I definitely would." The car had stopped at traffic lights. Thomson was readying to say something, but Rhodes was already reaching for the door handle.

"Take care of yourself, Spanner," he said as he got out.

Thomson watched as he strode towards the Jaguar and climbed in. The lights had changed to green, but a man was taking his time crossing the road, his movements resembling those of a marionette. Sheepskin coat, cap angled downwards over his forehead, newspaper tucked under one arm. Thomson leaned on the horn, but all the man did was flick the Vs. The performance, however, had given the Jaguar time to execute a three-point turn. Spanner Thomson rubbed a hand across his brow, put the car into first and carried on driving, his brain dizzy with permutations, as if Rhodes's horse race came with its own unique betting system, beyond the grasp of all but the most seasoned professional punter.

The man crossing the road in front of Spanner Thomson's car went by the name of Benny Mason, "Macey" to his many acquaintances. He was a small-time thief who had managed somehow not to take sides in a city that was all about which team you played for. Macey was on speaking terms with both John Rhodes and Cam Colvin—Matt Mason, too, if it came to it. He had checked but found no evidence of a blood tie between himself and Matt. Still, he could be useful for passing messages across the trenches, which was why he'd been approached a while back by DI Ernie Milligan, who'd shown him some files relating to unsolved housebreakings and the like before stating that he could have Macey dragged into court and found guilty on all charges.

"Even though I suspect you only did half of them."

He'd then bought Macey a drink and they'd come to an agreement, which was why Macey now sought a working phone box. After all, it wasn't every day you saw John Rhodes stepping from a car belonging to one of Cam Colvin's inner circle. No, that was a rare sighting indeed, which made it exactly the sort of thing Ernie Milligan would want to be made aware of, paying handsomely for the privilege . . .

21

It was Detective Inspector Ernest Milligan's belief that, Bobby Carter having been killed elsewhere before his body had been dumped, all business premises associated with Cam Colvin needed to be searched for bloodstains and Colvin himself brought in for questioning. Besides, a warning needed to be issued: no more attacks on John Rhodes's properties and employees. Commander Frederick had been insistent on that point.

So Milligan was not best pleased when his train of thought and his preparations were interrupted by word of a phone call. The caller refused to give a name and just said that he had something Milligan would want to hear. Finally Milligan relented and picked up the handset.

"DI Milligan here."

"About bloody time. I'm on my last bit of change."

Milligan recognised Macey's voice. "What have you got for me?"

"I've got John Rhodes getting out of Spanner Thomson's car on Castle Street."

Milligan was pulled up short. "You sure?"

"Well, I suppose I could have mistaken Jimmy Clitheroe for John Rhodes . . ."

"All right, smartarse. Any idea what was going on?"

"Rhodes had a Jag with a driver waiting. He got in and they left in the opposite direction from Thomson, leaving Spanner with a worried look on his face. It's got to be interesting, hasn't it?"

"Aye, maybe."

"By 'interesting,' I mean worth something."

"I'll see you right, Macey, fear not." Milligan slammed the phone down and scratched at his jaw. He stopped a passing DC. "Has Cam Colvin been brought in yet?"

"Should be here any minute."

"Let me know the second he's installed, and make sure he's in whichever interview room has the sewage problem."

"Understood."

Milligan caught sight of Laidlaw across the room. He made like a torpedo towards him. Laidlaw was sifting through the paperwork on his desk.

"Typing pool must have steam coming out of it," he said.

"Why aren't you in Balornock knocking on doors?"

"Because it's a waste of time."

"A waste of time that happens to be a direct order from your superior officer."

Laidlaw glowered at him. "If I ever start thinking of you as my superior in any way, shape or form, it'll be a sign I need to check into Gartnavel. By the way, have you done anything about Jenni Love?"

"Who?"

"The youngster Carter was cheating on his wife with."

"All in good time."

"She dances at a club called Whiskies. I've already checked it out and visited her home—proper policing rather than doorstepping."

"Did you meet her dad? I used to watch him when he played for the Gers."

"The Masonic lodge and Rangers FC—it's a wonder to me that you've scaled the giddy heights of CID. Anyway, Bob Lilley knows a bit more that might interest you, so if you pull him from the wild goose chase out at Springburn Park, you might not regret it." Laidlaw had finished browsing the sheets of paper. "Are you bringing in Colvin and his mob?"

"Just the main man to start with. But we're looking at his various businesses, especially workshops and scrapyards."

"Team's stretched as it is."

"Nevertheless." Milligan squared his shoulders.

Laidlaw leaned in towards him. "Every decision you make is being scrutinised upstairs. Any mistake, it's your name in red. You might try kicking the blame a rung or two down the ladder, but that won't wash with the people who count. My guess is, right now the newspapers, the council and all the local MPs are lining up to give the Commander a barracking, asking why the investigation's going nowhere while the city burns."

"That's why I'll be ordering Cam Colvin to cease hostilities." Milligan paused. "What if I told you John Rhodes and Spanner Thomson were seen sharing a car this morning?"

When Laidlaw seemed stymied for an answer, Milligan couldn't help but look pleased. "So while you're stuck in some sordid little investigation into the deceased's love life, the rest of us are focusing on the main event." He paused. "Might bring Archie Love in afterwards, though, just to get the measure of him."

"I don't think he knew about his daughter and Carter," Laidlaw warned.

"Well, telling him now's not going to make much difference, is it? It's not like he can go round the guy's house and give him a battering."

"Won't make the daughter's life any easier, though."

"I've always said you were too soft. Your head might be hard but your heart isn't." Milligan was being signalled to from across the room. "Looks like Cam Colvin's shown up."

"Want me in there with you when you question him?"

Milligan gave a snort and turned away.

"Thanks for considering it anyway," Laidlaw muttered.

There was a throbbing behind his temples. It had been there for the best part of an hour, growing steadily more insistent. "Not now, migraine," he told it. "I'll give you my full attention after work, I promise, but right now, I need to visit the Fourth Estate."

"Nice to see you've come tooled up, Cam," Milligan said as he entered the interview room.

The lawyer seated next to Cam Colvin wore a double breasted pinstripe suit and a burgundy-coloured silk tie. Slender red veins suffused his nose and cheeks. His name was Bryce Mundell, and Milligan had had plenty of dealings with him in the past. Bobby Carter's branch of the law was commercial, Mundell's criminal. If you were bent and could afford his fees, he was the man you went to. Yesterday he had been representing Spanner Thomson. It was no surprise to Milligan to be facing him again across the interview room table.

"The stink in here constitutes a health hazard," the lawyer complained, making show of unfurling a voluminous white cotton handkerchief and holding it to his nose and mouth.

"I wasn't aware of any smell until your client walked in," Milligan countered, getting comfortable.

"You're a regular Merry Mac fun page," Colvin told the detective.

"I like to brighten the gloom," Milligan agreed. "That's why I've got officers shining torches over each and every inch of real estate connected to you."

"I've been in touch with Commander Frederick about that," Mundell broke in, stuffing the handkerchief back into his pocket. "I'm far from convinced that proper procedures were followed before these searches commenced."

Milligan ignored this. His attention was on Colvin. "Setting light to the Gay Laddie is one sure way of bringing John Rhodes running. That what you want, Cam? Smacking two of his boys to the extent that both needed a hospital visit—still a wise move in hindsight?"

"I don't know what you're talking about." Colvin had folded his arms, head cocked to one side. He was peering at Milligan as though examining him on a slab. Milligan felt it was time for a bit of provocation. He opened the folder he'd brought with him. It was mostly for show, but he studied the topmost handwritten sheet while he counted off fifteen seconds. The solicitor was clicking his pen, indicating impatience. Not that he *would* be impatient, not when he billed by the quarter-hour.

"Was the meeting between Spanner and John Rhodes your idea?" Milligan asked, keeping his tone casual.

"What meeting?"

"Just over an hour ago."

Colvin shifted slightly in his chair. If his arms hadn't already been folded, Milligan reckoned the man would be crossing them now, unsettled and playing for time while the cogs turned.

"Spanner driving," Milligan continued into the silence, "Rhodes in the passenger seat, a nice chinwag going on. Not exactly subtle either—driving down Castle Street in the morning rush hour. Spotted by several witnesses, so you can take it from me that it happened. I'm just interested to know if it was done with your blessing. You spend half the night attacking Rhodes, then send Spanner—Spanner Thomson of all people—along for a parley." He broke off while he reconsidered. "Except that doesn't make sense, does it? They were driving into town from Balornock, meaning it was Rhodes who paid a call rather than the other way round. Even took the Jag and a driver with him so he could bail out before Spanner pushed too far into your neck of the woods."

He closed the folder again and tapped a finger against it. "Any comment, Cam?"

Mundell cleared his throat. "You're offering us nothing but hearsay, DI Milligan. My client has nothing to add."

Milligan opened the folder again and lifted out the front page of the previous day's evening paper. "This isn't exactly helpful."

Colvin studied the picture taken outside the Parlour. It was hard to tell if his attention was more on the widow or himself.

"In the absence of a press conference organised by the police," Mundell drawled in his expensively educated tones, "the victim's family decided to take matters into their own hands. Has any information been forthcoming as a result?"

"I'm not at liberty to say."

"Yesterday my client Mr. Thomson was shown a photofit relating to a person of possible interest seen near where the knife was discovered. Has there been any progress in identifying that individual?"

"We're not here about Spanner Thomson."

"Which begs the question, why *are* we here?" Mundell was glaring at Milligan.

"We're here because your client—today's client, I mean—could be in grave danger of starting a fairly messy war on the streets of my city. I need him to be aware of the consequences."

"It's John Rhodes you should be slapping down," Cam Colvin said.

"How about a meeting brokered between the two of you?"

"With a cop in the room, we'd have nothing to say." Colvin's eyes drilled into Milligan's. "And you'd want to be in that room, wouldn't you? No bragging rights otherwise. If Rhodes wants to talk, he knows where to find me. So far there's not been as much as a phone call or a card of condolence." He leaned back a little in his chair. "I hear tell Rhodes often stands a round or two of drinks at the Top Spot, including when Ben Finlay retired. Maybe that's your problem right there."

"Might my client have a point, DI Milligan?" Bryce Mundell

chipped in. "Mr. Colvin here has lost a good friend and business associate. It's odd that you're spending so much time harassing him and his colleagues while John Rhodes is allowed free rein. It almost smacks of favouritism. I'm quite sure you wouldn't want that allegation bandied about in the wider public sphere. Mud has a way of sticking, does it not?"

Milligan was aware of the colour creeping up his face. He closed the folder again and sprang to his feet.

"Can I take it we're finished here?" Mundell was trying not to smirk.

"Not by a long chalk," Milligan retorted, making his exit.

There was just the faintest bonfire aroma in the snug of the Gay Laddie. John Rhodes had summoned his two wounded soldiers there for a post-mortem. Not that either of them could offer much that he didn't already know. Their assailants had worn balaclavas, leaving only the eyes visible. Even then they'd picked their spot—a poorly lit street; a doorstep behind a tall hedge—leaving few if any possible witnesses. No words had been spoken at any point. The injuries sustained amounted to little more than bruising, a cracked rib and possible concussion. Rhodes hadn't bothered offering them an alcoholic beverage.

"Soft drinks are best for you boys," he had explained. A bottle of Lucozade had been unwrapped, uncapped and poured into half-pint glasses.

"Sorry if we let you down," one of the men had felt it necessary to say.

"You let your *guard* down, that's all. But that should be a lesson to you. Game we're in, it's never only nine to five. Your defence mechanism should never, ever be switched off, understood?"

There were nods from both men. They didn't even touch their drinks until a gesture from Rhodes told them they should.

Their first sip was wary, as if they suspected poison of some sort.

"I said we're in a game," Rhodes went on, "and that means we're a team. Someone hits us, we hit back. Don't think that's not coming. Don't think you won't be getting your revenge. But nothing rash, understood? It has to happen on *my* terms rather than yours, at a time of *my* choosing. I need you to know that I've not forgotten and I'm not ignoring you. It's just that something bigger might be brewing and there are things that need to be cleared up first."

"Whatever you say, Mr. Rhodes."

"We're just—"

Rhodes's right palm landed heavily on the table, causing both men to flinch.

"No more apologies," he said. "I don't want to hear them. I just want you to watch your backs in future, because this time you made it far too easy for whoever did this."

"It was Cam Colvin, surely."

"There's no 'surely' about it, son. Not in this business. Lazy thinking can lead you down any number of dead ends, and dead ends are where you're most likely to get jumped. Now bugger off, the pair of you." Rhodes reached into his pocket and brought out a couple of notes, sliding them across the table. "Let's call this sick pay," he said.

"We're not being given the boot?"

"You're on a warning, that's all. If you're savvy enough to learn from it, so much the better."

"On your way, lads," the scarred man said from behind them. They stood up, mumbling their thanks as they picked up the cash.

Once they'd gone, John Rhodes pushed his chair back and stretched out his legs.

"Maybe put them on overnight guard duty outside here," he said to the man with the scars.

"You think whoever hit the place will try again?"

"No, but do it anyway. It might dawn on them that it's by way of punishment. Then again it might not."

"The Lucozade was a nice touch."

"It's not because I care about them, if that's what you're thinking. It's because I'd sometimes be better off employing convalescent schoolkids. Though again, they might be too thick for the insult to get through. Now, do you need me to repeat any of my instructions?"

"Received and understood."

"Then what the hell are you waiting for? Go tell them!"

22

The Glasgow Press Club was on West George Street. A curving staircase—the bane of many an overweight journalist's life—led to a locked door behind which sat a bar and a separate snooker room. Eddie Devlin was already there. Devlin worked for the *Glasgow Herald* and had an archivist's knowledge of the city. A quarter-gill measure of whisky was waiting for Laidlaw, along with a jug of water. ATV was on in a corner of the room, showing what looked like an Open University programme.

"Barman's studying structural mechanics," Devlin explained. He had a pint of Tennent's in front of him, and would doubtless refer to his glass as half empty rather than half full.

"Get you a top-up?" Laidlaw asked, but the reporter shook his head. "I must be losing my hearing, Eddie," Laidlaw chided him.

"Doctor's orders. He wants me losing two stone. I did suggest he lop off a limb or two, but he advised against."

"What's the diagnosis?"

"You name it, I've got it. Diabetes, scarred lungs, coronary heart disease. Oh, and a touch of toothache too."

"Sounds like a full house to me. You're still working, though?"

"Crime never sleeps, Jack, and neither does the *Herald*'s chief reporter. Actually, I do snatch a few hours here and there, though I'm always fretting I might not wake up again. So fill me with good cheer—tell me you're here to divulge rather than dig."

"Sorry to disappoint you, Eddie." Laidlaw opened his cigarettes and offered Devlin one.

"I'm trying to quit." Which didn't stop him gazing wistfully at Laidlaw as he placed one between his lips and lit it.

"Willpower apart, what's the secret?"

"Polo mints and chewing gum."

"Explains the toothache, at any rate." In a small act of charity, Laidlaw blew some smoke his friend's way, watching Devlin inhale it. Then: "You hearing anything from your sources, Eddie?" He dragged the ashtray across the table towards him.

"About last night, you mean? One petrol bombing, two doings?"

"That and everything else. I'm sensing a pattern behind the chaos, but it's not quite revealed itself to me yet."

"You and me both. You know Carter wasn't the type to keep his nose clean? Had trouble keeping his trousers zipped, too."

"We've spoken to Jennifer Love. Are we missing any others?"

"Probably a slew of one-night stands and afternoon assignations. He'd go to that casino on Ingram Street. They have a couple of bedrooms on the top floor, sometimes used by clients when they're the worse for wear—I'm talking highrollers the casino treats with kid gloves. That's where Carter took at least some of his conquests."

"Seems like everybody knew except his wife and kids."

"Isn't that always the way of it, though?"

"Is the casino still run by Joey Frazer?"

"It's his name on the paperwork, but Colvin owns the building and takes the lion's share of the profits."

"So if Carter got in over his head . . ."

"Carter never did bet much. He'd eat a meal, drink a bottle of champagne, try a few spins of the wheel or hands of blackjack. It was just a place where he could socialise and maybe play the big man for the benefit of a secretary or hairdresser from Maryhill."

"Or a dancer from Knightswood."

Devlin's mouth twitched. "You know she was seeing Chick McAllister before Carter?"

"I've had a word with him."

"Then you'll know McAllister works for John Rhodes?"

"It's a small city, Eddie."

"You could paint it in a day," Devlin agreed. "But by the time you were finishing, there'd already be graffiti on the first bit."

The two men sat in silence for a moment, savouring their drinks. "Have you given any thought to Matt Mason?" Devlin eventually asked, his voice dropping several notches. Laidlaw looked at the other tables, pairs of men busy trading their own battle stories and tales of woe. No one seemed to be listening, but then none of them were daft either. They all knew who Laidlaw was, or at least what he was. When he spoke, Laidlaw's own voice had become a murmuring brook.

"Not especially. Are you saying we should?"

"You know who Jennifer Love's dad is?" Devlin watched Laidlaw give a slow nod. "Word is, Matt Mason pays his wages these days."

"What's the job description?"

"Love still knows a few people in the football world. He coaches youth teams, junior league. But those players often go on to bigger things, and through them Love meets pretty much anyone and everyone. There can be a lot of money riding on a game of football. A few bets spread across a variety of bookmakers, plus the pools, obviously."

"You're saying Love talks players into chucking the odd game?"

Devlin offered a shrug. "Goalkeepers are the easiest route. A busy goalmouth, a fumbled catch, maybe something that makes your defenders look equally culpable. I'm not saying it's true, but it's what I've been hearing."

"And meantime Love's daughter switches from one of John Rhodes's men to one of Cam Colvin's."

"Can you see her father being thrilled about that when he's tied his wagon to Matt Mason's horse?"

"I can't, no. Thanks for that, Eddie."

"Anything for me in return?"

"Milligan's being the usual bull in a china shop."

"Isn't that your role?"

"He's pulled in Cam Colvin for a word."

"Stands to reason after the attack on the Gay Laddie."

"Much good it'll do him."

"Remember me telling you I'm a sick man, Jack? This is hellish thin gruel you're feeding me."

"I thought you were trying to lose weight, Eddie."

"I'd rather not lose my job at the same time. Newspapers don't look good with big white gaps where the stories should be. If I don't give my boss something soon, I might have to emigrate."

"I hear South Africa's nice."

"Might explain why they're taking out so many ads in the paper." Devlin gave Laidlaw a look. "But then you already know that."

"Because I read it religiously, Eddie. Nice to see Mr. Heath's keen on us joining the Common Market. I hear Enoch Powell was in town recently, stirring up shit." He saw Devlin wince. "You were there?"

"Editor's orders."

"Then you're every bit as well informed as me," he offered by way of apology. "I'll happily let you trounce me at a frame of snooker if that would help ease the discomfort."

"I've seen you play snooker, Jack. I could read Proust in the original French in less time than it takes you to pot a ball."

"But only be half as entertained in the process," Laidlaw said, raising his emptied glass in a mock toast.

23

C olvin had gathered his men in the same function room at the Coronach Hotel, Dan Tomlinson providing alcohol-free drinks only. Panda Paterson would look in vain for snacks, Colvin having instructed Tomlinson to keep catering to a minimum. Colvin sat at the head of the table, producing a freshly laundered hankie and blowing his nose before starting to speak.

"First thing to say is, it's good to have you back, Spanner. I trust you were treated well at Central Division."

"I gave them nothing because there was nothing to give," Thomson said.

Colvin nodded his apparent acceptance. "They doled me out the exact same treatment," he said, "albeit for different reasons. Seemed to think I might have sanctioned the attack on the Gay Laddie and those two punishment beatings. The word is, Rhodes's men are giving Milligan's team nothing, but didn't actually see who it was that jumped them anyway." He paused to play with one of his gold cufflinks. "I can understand the impulse to do *something*, maybe thinking it would make a nice gift for me, tied with a ribbon and everything, but that's not the way things work. So which one of you arseholes was it?"

The four men exchanged glances and shrugs.

"I'm inclined to rule out Spanner, not that he was in custody at the time, but cops were probably keeping an eye on him. Mickey, Dod and Panda—ball's in your penalty box, so to speak."

"Nothing to do with me," Ballater muttered, while his colleagues shook their heads in agreement.

"Someone further down the ranks then," Colvin offered. "I need you to find out who. Start with the eager beavers, the ones keenest to please you. They're going to want to be found out, thinking it'll mean a promotion, or at the very least a peck on the cheek."

"Have you considered Matt Mason, boss?" Dod Menzies asked.

"I've considered *everything*, Dod," Colvin snapped back. "What is it about me that makes you think I wouldn't have?"

Menzies held both palms out in a show of surrender. "Just saying, if anyone stands to gain from you and Rhodes squaring up to one another . . ."

"Guessing games are all well and good, but it's answers I need and you lot sitting around here on your fat arses isn't bringing me them." Colvin fixed each man in turn with a look. "So get out there and get asking." As the four of them started rising to their feet, he turned his head towards Thomson. "Hang back a minute, Spanner," he ordered. "I want to compare notes with you about Ernie Milligan."

Colvin dribbled some more water into his glass as the others shuffled out, Paterson intimating to Thomson that they would wait in the car. Once the door was closed, Colvin waited another half-minute before giving Spanner Thomson his full and undivided attention.

"What about Milligan?" Thomson asked into the silence.

"Anything you want to tell me, Spanner? Anything you might know that I don't?"

Thomson shook his head warily.

"I'm talking about this morning rather than yesterday."

Thomson's shoulders slumped perceptibly. "John Rhodes," he said in an undertone.

"Not very clandestine, was it? Driving down Castle Street in broad daylight. So what did he want?"

"He thinks me getting pulled in might change things."

"What things?"

"You and me, me and the others." Thomson jerked his head in the direction of the door.

"And you planned on keeping this to yourself?"

"I knew how it would look. How it *does* look. But John Rhodes is going to get nothing from me, that's a promise."

"I'm glad to hear it, because if you ever tried crossing me, I'd go after your whole family, from long-buried ancestors to third cousins twice removed that you didn't even know you had. Understood?"

"Christ's sake, Cam, how long have we known one another?"

Colvin struck the table with the flat of his hand. "That counts for fuck all, Spanner." He had bared his teeth, matching the ferocity of his tone. "Anyone comes for me, I drop the atomic bomb on them. Are we clear on that?"

Thomson nodded sullenly.

"Anything else to tell me about our friend Rhodes?"

"He was waiting around the corner from my house."

"He wouldn't have wanted the neighbours seeing. Even so, his presence in your company was noted, meaning he wasn't too bothered about keeping it quiet. He's playing games with us, Spanner, I hope you appreciate that. I've known you longer than just about anyone in my life. If Rhodes can drive a wedge between us, he reckons he can do anything."

Thomson couldn't quite bring himself to make eye contact. "He told me Bobby was planning to jump ship and set up for himself. In competition, I mean."

Colvin gave a snort. "He told you that, aye?"

"He also said it's the sort of thing we'd expect him to say."

"John Rhodes wasn't at the back of the queue when rank animal cunning was being handed out by the man upstairs."

"You think he was spinning me a line? I know you put a lot of trust in Bobby, Cam, but the rest of us didn't quite see the same golden boy you did . . ."

Colvin's face darkened further. "Bobby was one of us, no matter what poison John Rhodes spouts. You'd do well to remember that."

"Yes, Cam."

"So if and when he contacts you again . . . ?"

"I come straight to you."

"Fucking right you do. And don't you ever try keeping something like this from me again." Colvin paused. "And if you have any inkling who gave the nod for those hits last night . . ."

"Swear to God I don't."

"Then get out there and find out who it was!"

Thomson sprang to his feet, but paused after a couple of steps. "Are we okay, Cam?"

"You tell me, Spanner."

"I'd hate for us not to be." He waited a further moment, but his boss was busying himself with his cufflinks again.

As Thomson yanked open the door, he saw Mickey Ballater a few yards down the corridor. Ballater started striding towards him.

"Need a word with the chief," he explained. "I'll see you in the car."

Thomson nodded and left, Ballater entering the room and closing the door behind him.

"Everything okay, Cam?" he enquired.

"Something I can do for you, Mickey?"

"Just wanted to make sure there's not a problem with you and Spanner. If there is, you only have to ask."

Colvin pressed his hands together, fingertips to his lips. "I might need you to keep an eye on him for me. He had John Rhodes in his car this morning. If that happens again, I want to hear about it from one of my own guys rather than CID."

"What did Rhodes want?"

"Most probably us fighting each other rather than him."

"But you're not sure you can trust Spanner?"

Colvin made a non-committal gesture.

"The knife was planted near Spanner's home," Ballater went on. "Next thing, John Rhodes is paying a visit. I'd say Rhodes fancies Spanner for the killing and wants us to know it."

"Or he's covering for one of his own. You know Jenni Love and Chick McAllister used to be an item?"

"That was a while back, though. And she'd broken things off with Bobby before he got done in."

"Jealousy's weird, though, isn't it? It's not rational the way business is. When we pay a visit to someone, it's always because of business. It's never personal. Whenever I've seen anyone make a mess of things, it's because they let the heart rule the head and they stopped thinking."

"Chick McAllister doesn't have the shortest of fuses."

"He might harbour grudges, though, letting them fester quietly deep down."

"In which case he's the one we should be watching, rather than Spanner."

"One step at a time, Mickey. Eyes on Spanner, find out who was busy last night, and after that we can focus on McAllister—agreed?"

"One hundred per cent, Cam."

Colvin stretched an arm out so it rested along the back of the empty chair next to him. He didn't have to say anything. The meaning was loud and clear and Mickey Ballater nodded his complete comprehension and acceptance of the implicit offer.

In the otherwise empty hotel car park, Menzies, Paterson

and Thomson had the engine running so the heating was on. The Peugeot 504 was a big car, but they filled it—Menzies behind the wheel, Thomson in the passenger seat, Paterson in the back. Their eyes were on the hotel entrance, wondering what Mickey Ballater was up to.

"Can we trust him?" Menzies asked.

"He's hungry," Thomson answered. "And he thinks he's smart."

"Neither of you had anything to do with last night?" Paterson asked before taking another bite of his macaroon bar.

"I know I didn't."

"Me neither. How about you, Panda?"

Paterson chewed and swallowed before replying. "I wouldn't put it past Mickey, though. He likes to surround himself with the youngsters, showing off to them. I'm sure one or two would jump if he told them to. If he wants to go question any of them without us being there, that might be a sign that he needs us kept away from them in case they let something slip."

There were nods of agreement from the front seats.

"I might as well tell you," Thomson added, "that I had a visit from John Rhodes this morning. He says he wants to be my buddy."

Dod Menzies snorted, kneading the steering wheel. His hands were gloved, the gloves a gift from his wife. They were made of the thinnest, softest leather, with a button to keep them nice and tight around the wrists. He always wore them when driving, and when carrying out various other tasks too.

"Cam knows you're not Judas material," Paterson assured Thomson, stuffing the empty sweet wrapper into his coat pocket.

"Even though you're just about daft enough to have done Bobby in and tossed the knife into a bush practically outside your back door." Menzies gave a chuckle.

"Don't even joke about it," Thomson said with a scowl. "It feels like somebody's doing a decent job of stitching me up here." He rubbed at his chest, feeling the comforting weight of the concealed spanner.

"As if you'd use a blade," Paterson said, gripping the back of the passenger seat and pulling himself forward. "We all know Mickey's the one who likes a proper knife."

"Though he prefers a razor," Menzies countered. "Besides, Mickey's not the one with the hots for the widow."

"Don't be too sure about that," Thomson said quietly.

"How do you mean, Spanner?"

Thomson just shrugged, all three of them watching as Ballater emerged from the building, pulling up his collar and almost dancing down the steps towards them. He seemed relaxed, as if his little chat with Cam Colvin were a job interview that had gone exceedingly well. He didn't even look particularly put out that he was being consigned to the back seat. He climbed in and closed the door.

"Everything all right?" Menzies enquired, watching in the rear-view mirror.

"Right as rain," Ballater answered, clapping his hands together and rubbing them. "So are we going to make a few house calls or what?"

"Just like the boss said."

"Mind you, it'll take us all day if we don't divvy it up," Ballater commented. "I could talk to my guys while you talk to yours."

"Maybe that's what we'll do then," Menzies said, releasing the handbrake and giving Spanner Thomson the most meaningful of looks.

24

There were goalposts but no nets and the turf had been churned by a succession of studded boots. Discarded jackets took the place of corner flags and line markings existed only in the imaginations of those present. Pulpy leaves covered the stretch of parkland where Laidlaw emerged from the line of trees. The sky was almost as sullen as the smattering of spectators. Red plastic Adidas shoulder bags were lined up next to the pitch. Beside them stood three men in matching tracksuits, shouting instructions and imprecations towards the teenage boys whose field of dreams this purported to be.

Laidlaw recognised Archie Love, who was a good couple of decades older than the assistants flanking him. The other onlookers comprised parents and bored siblings, some of whom were busy exercising their dribbling skills.

"Fuck's sake, Kenny, Stevie Wonder could have made that tackle!" Love spat the words with real passion, his arms outstretched. He slapped his palms against his thighs in exasperation.

"The boy's weary," one of the assistants offered by way of excuse.

"Too many copies of *Mayfair* hidden in his bedroom," the other agreed. "Right arm's getting more exercise than the rest of him put together."

"You'd know all about that, Jimmy," Love complained, "seeing how you're the source of most of those mags."

"Man has to make a living, Archie."

"Mr. Love?"

All three turned at the sound of Laidlaw's voice.

"Sorry to drag you away from an enthralling encounter, but could I have a minute of your time?"

Love checked his wristwatch. "Forty-five's nearly up anyway." There was a tin whistle hanging around his neck. He puckered his lips around it and blew. There were groans of relief as the players started making for the touchline.

"Sort them out," Love commanded before heading in the direction of the trees and the footpath beyond. He was about six inches shorter than Laidlaw, and he'd added maybe a stone and a half in weight since his playing days. The thick head of hair was turning silver, his tan showing that he still treated himself to overseas holidays.

"What's this about?" he asked, unwrapping a stick of gum and readying to place it in his mouth. He changed his mind, however, when Laidlaw produced a pack of cigarettes. "Give me one of those, will you?" Laidlaw obliged and the uneaten gum was tossed onto the grass. Both men smoked in silence for a moment.

"I'm a detective, Mr. Love."

"I didn't think you were a scout from Inter Milan, son."

"I did play a bit in my younger days. A few folk said I was good enough to stick at it."

"So what happened?"

"I decided not to waste my life playing games. Speaking of scouting, though, you do a bit yourself, I hear."

"Good young players are rarer than a convent with the toilet seat up. I sometimes steer one towards a deal that's going to be right for him, then I'm left to watch as most of them piss it all away. Talent *and* brains is the rarest combination of all." Love studied Laidlaw above the cigarette in his mouth, having offered him all he was going to get by way of casual conversation.

"Do you know a man called Matt Mason, Mr. Love?"

"By reputation."

"You've never done any work for him."

"That's a pretty wild allegation to be making. How about telling me your name, for when I make my complaint?"

"It's Detective Constable Laidlaw. You'll find me at Central Division, where I'm investigating the murder of Bobby Carter. I don't suppose you knew him?"

"Bobby Carter?" Love shook his head and checked his watch. Some of the players were stretched out on the edge of the playing field, as if a soft bed couldn't come soon enough. Love blew on the whistle, gesturing for his assistants to get them back on their feet.

"I'm not doing too well here, am I?" Laidlaw said. "Let's try one final name—Chick McAllister."

"He's a friend of my daughter's."

"Her boyfriend, in fact, at one time."

Love gave a shrug.

"Were you aware that he works for John Rhodes?"

"The laddie seemed fine, very respectful."

"But not exactly son-in-law material?"

"My Jennifer's too young for any of that."

"That's the problem, though, isn't it? She's not going to remain yours for much longer. She's got her own life to lead and decisions she'll want to make without any interference from you and her mum." Laidlaw paused as the man's face grew taut. "I speak as a parent myself."

"What exactly are you doing here?"

"How do you feel about the fact that Jennifer works as a dancer?"

"How would *you* feel?"

"I imagine I'd be a bit fearful. Mine are a good bit younger, so there are a few more cotton-wool years left."

"Dancing's all she does, you know. She knows better than to go with any of the lowlifes who stand there staring at her."

"You've watched her, then?"

A momentary discomfort passed across Love's face, as though he'd been found out. "What kind of father wouldn't want to check out the place where his daughter works?"

"Most of them, I'd say."

"Maybe you'll find out some day, when yours have grown."

"You sound far from happy about her chosen career, Mr. Love. And as for her not hanging out with the punters . . ."

"What?"

Laidlaw hadn't known until this point that he was about to say anything. Later, he would wonder why he had, knowing it was bound to cause an angry scene in the Love household. He suspected it was because he had taken an immediate and visceral dislike to the man. It was to do with his attitude, the way his living room was focused on *him*—his chair, his memorabilia. He didn't doubt that Love's wife had been ground down by years spent under his control. Meantime, Laidlaw had a knife of sorts, and he couldn't help but twist it.

"Jenni was seeing Bobby Carter, Mr. Love," he revealed. "This was after she broke up with McAllister. Carter worked for Cam Colvin, McAllister belongs to John Rhodes, and I hear whispers Matt Mason has you tucked in his breast pocket like one of those fake cardboard pocket-chiefs you can buy at the Barras." Examining the effect of his words, Laidlaw reached the swift conclusion that Carter was coming as news to Jenni's father, so much so that there wasn't room in his head for a denial of his links to Mason.

"I would have known," he said quietly.

"Would you, though? Is that the sort of relationship you've fostered with your daughter, Mr. Love? Or is it more likely your family hide things from you to stop you taking off like a saturn rocket?"

A cry came from the touchline, one of the assistants tapping his wrist.

"Lucky for you I have to go," Love growled.

"You can swear to me you didn't know about Jenni and Bobby Carter? If you had, what would you have done?"

"All depends, doesn't it?"

"You'd have had words at the very least, though? Maybe at a rendezvous like the Parlour?"

"The Parlour's a John Rhodes pub."

"As Matt Mason's man, you wouldn't have been comfortable there?"

"I'm my own man and nobody else's." Love showed his teeth as he spoke. Laidlaw was shaking his head slowly.

"You're bought and sold for a gangster's shilling," he corrected him. "In my book that gives you all the integrity of a back-street hoor at chucking-out time."

He watched as the man squared his shoulders and clenched his fists. One appraising look at his opponent, however, was enough to change Love's mind. Instead, he began to trudge back towards his other family. Laidlaw wondered if he really deserved either of them, but then the world both men inhabited was seldom equitable that way.

25

W ell," Bob Lilley said, "what did you make of that?"
Margaret went up through the gears. It was her turn
to drive. She'd had just the one glass of warmish
white. Bob had enjoyed a lot more, as well as a large post-pran-
dial helping of Antiquary.

"Lovely kids," Margaret answered. "Shame they're living
on a battlefield."

"That's a bit over the top."

"Maybe. They're good people, but there's so much tension
in that house. Don't tell me you didn't feel it?"

"I became progressively more inoculated."

Margaret enjoyed driving at this time of night, when the city
dozed and the only hindrance was the occasional red light or
tipsy pedestrian. She had never told Bob this, however. It
would only have given him the excuse to avoid his turn at the
wheel—and she enjoyed a drop of wine as much as she enjoyed
being in the driver's seat.

"Anyway," he said, "tell me more."

She knew he was aware that she read domestic situations
more astutely than he did, although that knowledge didn't
always sit easily with him. He'd said himself more than once
that she'd have made a good detective.

"Every marriage has its darker moments," she obliged.
"Even ours. But we tend to bury the corpses and get on with
things. Tonight, I thought some of them were sitting with us at
the table. When we were talking about the hours you boys put

in and I said you've been told that if you're coming home after midnight you've to take the couch so you don't wake me up . . ."

"And Ena said Laidlaw prefers to stay out."

"It was what she said afterwards, though, about it being like having a soldier who only ever comes home on leave." Margaret paused. "I'm guessing something's happened and that's why she was keen to have us round. She needs to feel she has witnesses. Does Jack play the field?"

"I've not long met the man," Lilley argued, before proffering a sigh to fill the silence. "He sleeps some nights in a hotel in town; says it's so he can stay close to whatever he's investigating."

"He's a good-looking man, though."

"You think so? I hope you're not getting interested."

She laughed and placed her free hand on his thigh. "I'm spoken for. Besides, he's too dangerous."

"And I'm not?"

"Maybe he's a different type of dangerous—there were moments I could sense him ticking like a bomb. More than that, it was as if Ena *wanted* him to explode, so we'd see what she has to deal with. Did you not feel that, Bob?"

"Maybe she's not worked out yet who it is she married."

"Has he even worked that out himself?"

"Let's say he's a work in progress, then, and thank our lucky stars we're past all that."

"Did I not say? I'm leaving you next week."

"Mind and take the mortgage with you." Lilley smiled as he did some thinking. "You're right in one respect—it was awkward seeing him in his home setting, like he wasn't comfortable there. Maybe he's a streetsman, the way Davy Crockett was a woodsman. Davy could read all the signs in the wild, he'd lived there so long. Probably wasn't so good on the domestic front. I think Jack's like that with Glasgow: he brings the city home with him, and that's too much for even a decent-sized living room to contain."

Margaret seemed to be considering his words as she slowed, the lights ahead changing to red. "Bit of a romanticised notion you've got of him, no?"

"I think he *is* a romantic, in a weird sort of way. He really believes there's truth to be found on the streets that exists nowhere else."

They watched as two men weaved down the pavement, their heated discussion conducted in nothing but curses and adverbs.

"Do you want to deal with that?" Margaret asked.

"I'm off duty. Besides, that's not a fight, it's a decibel contest. Look at the bellies on the pair of them—they're like Lambeg drums, big and noisy but with nothing but air inside."

"You're even beginning to speak like him," Margaret said with an indulgent smile.

The lights changed to green and they set off again.

"Another thing about Jack is, he's deep," Lilley went on. "I got no sense of that from the house—everything in there seemed to be more Ena's than his. On his desk at work he has these foreign books. Spanish, French, Danish maybe. Philosophers. Yet all I saw in the living room was Catherine Cookson."

"He's in hiding, then, is that what you're saying?"

"I've not known him nearly long enough to form a view." Lilley paused. "We're going to have to return the favour, aren't we? Invite them round to ours?"

"Would that be such a bad thing? Maybe away from the kids they can find out what it is they like about one another." Margaret paused, moving up through the gears. "Then again, in public they've maybe perfected the happy families act. Could be that's why the meal had to be on her territory, masks removed."

"You really think she wants us on her side and not his?"

"I doubt there's room in that marriage for neutrals."

"And have you decided whose colours you'll be wearing."

"Hers, obviously."

"Even though he's a good-looking man, and a romantic with it?"

"Never bet against the wife, Bob. You should know that by now. Speaking of which, I'm going to bed when we get in, and you're fetching me a cup of tea and maybe a wee brandy."

"Yes, ma'am," Lilley said, giving a salute as Margaret squeezed his thigh again.

"Are we the only people we know who've not seen that film?" Ena asked as she busied herself washing the dishes.

"You don't do X certificates, remember. Even a musical like *Cabaret*."

"Al Pacino's supposed to be very good, though." She glanced towards Laidlaw, who was drying the wine glasses. "They seem nice, don't they?"

"Salt of the earth."

"You once told me armies salt the earth to stop crops growing."

"Well, that's true." Laidlaw opened a cupboard door.

"Next one along for glasses," Ena informed him.

"It's been a while," he said. Then: "Why exactly did you invite them?"

"Any reason why not?"

"It's just unusual, that's all."

"Inviting people to dinner?"

"*Us* having people to dinner. It's all a bit . . ."

"Middle class? Did I miss you cleaning the coal dust from under your fingernails before we sat down?"

"I'm not much of a one for small talk, you know that."

"Which explains why you didn't say much of anything."

"I kept smiling, though, didn't I? And I talked about the kids."

"You don't get extra marks for doing something any father would do without having to think twice about it."

"Maybe that's because most people don't think before they speak. As a result, most of what passes for conversation is just dross. Sifting through it is what gives me those dirty nails." He saw the look she was giving him. "Present company excepted, obviously. Your conversation is always the stuff of legend." He snatched up a couple of plates with the dish towel.

"When you've done those, can you bring the bowls through?"

He nodded and complied. There wasn't a separate dining room, but the living room was big enough for a large dropleaf table and four chairs. He started piling up the pudding bowls, while struggling to think back to what the starter had been. He paused and looked around him. Two armchairs and a matching floral sofa; framed photos of the three children on the wall unit; china ornaments that had belonged to Ena's mother—there had been only one casualty so far due to the kids. A smoked-glass bowl sat on top of the unit, a ceramic cat attached to its rim, eyes locked on a smaller ceramic mouse inside. There was a tiny amount of Antiquary still in Laidlaw's glass, so he finished it, rinsing it around his mouth. In the past, he had tried reading the meaning behind the bowl and the scene playing out on and within it. Was he the cat or the mouse? Was the bowl Ena's idea of their marriage? Or did she just think it a charming and witty addition to the room?

He was all too aware that he had been neither charming nor witty during the meal. But he'd been placid, she couldn't say he hadn't been that. Placid *and* polite.

Though, as she had already indicated, he deserved extra marks for neither.

"Are you stopping here tonight?" Ena asked. She was standing in the doorway, suds on her hands.

"I've got another early start."

"There's an alarm clock, Jack."

In the end, he offered the nodded acceptance that the situation seemed to require.

"Fine then," his wife said, turning away from him again.

"I'll just go up and check on the kids," he said, conscious that she had stopped listening. On the staircase, his legs felt simultaneously heavier and lighter with each step he climbed.

Four in the morning. That was the Faron Young song, wasn't it? *Four in the morning and . . .* something about the dawning. Not dawn yet in Glasgow, though, as the passenger climbed out of the car. The driver stayed, ready to give warning, engine ticking over. The fence was high, the gates secured by a heavy chain and padlock. He hoisted the bolt cutters but froze as a man in a stained car coat appeared around the corner, looking almost concussed. Either one of the local prozzies had given him a doing, or he'd passed out from the night's bevvy and dozed on the pavement until the chill shook him awake. The passer-by saw the bolt cutters a moment before raising his eyes to the figure who was releasing them. That figure now reached into a pocket, producing a combat knife, which came with a serrated edge and a nasty-looking tip.

"Keep walking and you'll keep breathing. Open your mouth about this and you'll find it widened by a fair few inches when I catch up with you—got that, or would a few wee nicks maybe help you file it away?"

The pedestrian didn't need telling, his eyes fixed on the knife that was being flexed in front of him.

"None of my business, son, God's honest truth." The man began stumbling away. The driver was watching his colleague intently. A shake of the head as the knife was tucked back into pocket said no further action need be taken. Not this time. He bent down and retrieved the bolt cutters.

Four in the morning: how did the tune go again? He'd maybe get them to play it in Whiskies. It was a bit mournful, but who was going to stop him? And if anyone could dance to it, that wee ride Jenni could . . .

Day Five

E

xplains why I had trouble getting a taxi," Laidlaw said to Lilley.

They were standing on the pavement next to a high mesh fence topped with strands of barbed wire. The padlock on the gates had been cut and lay on the ground. Inside the compound sat a dozen black cabs, their tyres slashed and windshields smashed. Laidlaw examined the surrounding buildings—disused warehouses and single-storey factory units.

"Only likely witnesses that time of night would be tarts and their clients," Lilley commented, "judging by the johnnies strewn along the gutters."

"You paint a compelling picture, Bob."

Crime-scene officers were dusting for prints and shooting roll upon roll of film. Laidlaw dislodged a sliver of bacon from between his teeth and flicked it towards the ground.

"Hotel again last night?" Lilley enquired. He watched Laidlaw shake his head. "Thanks for the meal, by the way."

"Don't feel under any compunction to invite us round to yours too soon."

"Understood."

"I hope Cam Colvin's premiums are up to date. Who fronts the place for him?"

"Betty Fraser." Lilley watched one of Laidlaw's eyebrows rise a fraction. "A rare enough commodity, I know, but she's driven cabs for twenty years, knows her stuff, and her drivers are loyal to her."

"Meaning they don't skim too much off each fare? Was the business always hers?"

Lilley nodded. "Colvin came in as a sleeping partner three or four years back. Seems he made her an offer she—"

"I get the picture, Bob." The two detectives were walking around the inner perimeter of the compound, so as not to get in the way.

"Tit for tat, isn't it?" Lilley commented.

"And if the damage is covered by insurance, the only thing hurt is Colvin's pride."

"You reckon John Rhodes is good for it?"

"Maybe."

"Just maybe?"

"Just maybe," Laidlaw echoed.

"So what does Colvin do now?"

"He either sits on his hands or he escalates."

"Would it do any good to put the two of them in a room together?"

"Only if you run a funeral business." Laidlaw was lighting a cigarette. There were only two left in the packet, and he needed new flints for his lighter. "Any chance I can hitch a lift?"

Lilley checked his watch. "We could grab a cuppa first—there's another forty minutes before the morning briefing."

"I'm not going to the morning briefing, Bob."

"How far do you think you can push Milligan before the top of his head comes off?"

"It's an ongoing experiment."

"So where am I giving you a lift to?"

"First stop's a tobacconist, Bearsden after that."

"You're going to see the widow?"

Laidlaw shook his head. "I thought I'd drop in on a convalescing friend."

Lilley worked it out in a matter of seconds. "Matt Mason's out of hospital?"

"The very man," Laidlaw said.

"Am I invited?"

"Not really."

"Thanks a lot."

"It's for your own good. If Milligan gets to hear that I'm freelancing, best that you can deny all knowledge."

"Except that I'm supposed to be babysitting you—and that's the Commander's orders rather than Ernie Milligan's."

"You really think I need babysitting, Bob?"

"What you need, Jack, is nothing short of a guardian bloody angel."

Matt Mason's home was an unassuming bungalow on a quiet street of well-kept flower beds and windows shielded by net curtains. Unassuming or no, it would be worth north of ten thousand pounds in this part of town. A Ford Escort RS1600 was parked on the road outside, while the driveway itself was empty. It was a conspicuous car, and intended to be so. Laidlaw tapped on the driver's-side window and waited while the scowling figure within deigned to wind it down.

"The name's Detective Constable Laidlaw. Just here for a word with your boss, no dramatics needed."

"I'm waiting to pick up a pal."

"Of course you are, and so is the bulge under your armpit. It better fire nothing more deadly than caps, or I might need to haul you out of there and into a Black Maria." While he waited for his words to sink in, he looked up and down the empty street. "Any reason for Matt to feel the need for more firepower than usual? This thing you're sat in is about as subtle as a tricolour at Ibrox." The driver wasn't about to answer, so Laidlaw turned away, passed through the wrought-iron gate and rang the doorbell.

The woman who answered wore a floral apron and was wiping her hands on a dish towel.

"Mrs. Mason? I'm here to see Matt."

"Is he expecting you?"

"I was hoping for the element of surprise." Laidlaw held up his warrant card and she dropped the impersonation of suburban housewife, her face becoming stony, eyes as cold as any mugger's.

"He's just out of hospital."

"Which is why I'm here and not there."

"Have you got a search warrant?"

"I'm only after a talk with the man, unless you think there's something more serious I should be exploring?"

She half turned, as if to assure herself nothing incriminating was within view.

"Matt won't be happy," she stated. "He keeps family and business separate."

"That's nice. Through here, aye?" Laidlaw began to squeeze past her. It was a calculated risk. One gesture from her and the gorilla in the car would come bounding up the path. But as he walked down the hall, his feet making no discernible sound as they stepped on a good half-inch depth of expensive-looking pale carpet, he heard the door behind him click shut. He glanced into the living room as he passed it. The voluminous three-piece suite looked new. Maybe there'd been a trip to Carrick Furniture.

"He's in the garden," she called out. "Through the dining room extension."

Matt Mason was dressed for the weather, a fleecy jacket zipped to his neck and a flat cap on his head. Beneath the cap, the hair was thinning. He wasn't much over five feet two in height, stocky with it. He sat at a round metal table, a walking stick propped next to him. The morning paper was open at the sports pages, alongside an empty mug.

"I see Colin Stein's leaving Rangers," Laidlaw said.

"Who the hell are you?" Mason responded, watching as

Laidlaw dragged out the chair opposite and sat himself down.

"I'm CID. The name's Laidlaw."

"It's a name I've heard."

"Just wanted to check that there's no good news. You being up and about confirms it."

"You're the owner of a smart mouth, Laidlaw. You want to be careful how you drive it though."

"A bit like one of Cam Colvin's taxis, eh? Some garage proprietor is going to be popping the champagne and booking a week in the sunshine."

"I take it he got hit?"

"Don't pretend it's coming as news to you."

"It is, though."

Laidlaw shook his head slowly. "It's not John Rhodes's style, and Colvin isn't canny enough to attack his own business so he could lay the blame on the opposition. You, though . . ." He jabbed a finger towards Mason. "Seems to me you've got most to gain from Colvin and Rhodes fighting each other."

"Is that right?"

"Feel free to correct me if I'm wrong."

Mason considered for a moment. "No, you're probably right. All the same, I didn't do anything to Colvin's taxis. They belong to Betty Fraser, and I like Betty. I knew her father back in the day. She's the one losing money while the cabs are being fixed. Colvin will still demand his cut at month's end."

Laidlaw was breaking the seal on a fresh packet of cigarettes. He paused. "If you don't mind?" he said. It was a small concession, but a concession nonetheless. Mason acknowledged as much with his eyes.

"Puff away," he said.

Laidlaw used his lighter. The tobacconist had changed its flint and topped up the gas.

"That's a nice one," Mason said, admiring it.

"Present from my brother. He didn't like that I used to be fitter than him. Decided to hobble me by facilitating my habit."

Mason smiled a thin smile. "What are you really doing here?"

"Just getting a feel for things." Laidlaw took in his surroundings. "All your own work?"

"We've got a gardener."

"Bearsden seems to be the place, eh? For men going up in the world, I mean. Cam Colvin's not too far away, and Bobby Carter had recently moved into the vicinity. I know you grew up in the Gallowgate; not the easiest of upbringings. Yet here you are, and that's what separates the likes of you and Colvin from John Rhodes."

"Because Rhodes still lives in the Calton? You think that makes him—what?—more authentic?" Mason gave a sneer. "To my mind it makes him lazy. His world's shrinking around him and he can't even see it."

"Whereas you and Colvin are always hungry for more—more power, more money, more territory?"

"It's called capitalism, Laidlaw."

"Not the way you do it. Your style is more totalitarian regime with punishment beatings and disappearances. History isn't on your side."

"In which case I say: fuck history."

"That'll look perfect on your headstone. Seen much of Archie Love lately?"

"Who?"

"What drugs did they give you in hospital, Matt? They seem to have affected your brainpan. Love's the guy who gets players to throw games so you can make the extra few quid you so sorely don't need while heaping on them a lifetime of guilt and self-loathing. He's also the father of Jenni Love, who was seeing Bobby Carter on the fly. Ringing any bells now? You might have thought you were doing Love a favour by getting rid of Carter. Maybe you didn't know Jenni had split up with him. Maybe you thought you'd be wrapping your tentacles around her father that bit tighter, so he wouldn't suddenly get cold feet. And wouldn't it be grand if Carter's death could in some way be pinned either on John Rhodes or one of Cam Colvin's own team?"

Laidlaw broke off, studying Mason's face as if he were a surgeon about to operate on its owner. "I'm just wondering if you're clever enough to have thought all that through, and now that I've seen you in the flesh, I'm having grave doubts. Very grave doubts. Added to which, the armed guard out front tells me you think you're under threat. Question is: who from? I doubt you're going to tell me. In fact, I'd guess you don't really know. If you did, you'd have felt compelled to do something noisy and public about it. So there you are, that's why I came here—like I said, to get a feel for things." He rose to his feet.

"How long have you been in the police?" Mason asked.

"Long enough."

"What was it about the job that attracted you?"

"The privilege of studying human nature close up. That and the pension plan."

Mason managed another thin smile. "See, most cops I meet, there's not much behind the eyes, your boss Ernie Milligan being a prime example, but you strike me as different."

"Flattery will get you nowhere, Mr. Mason."

"I'm not flattering you, son, but you already know that. You've a good enough conceit of yourself. You know your strengths, but remember to watch out for your weaknesses, too."

"And what might those be?"

"I think you're maybe a bit more idealistic than you let on. You believe in things like justice and fair play."

"And you've culled all of that from our chat here today? You should open a psychiatric practice."

"One more thing, then. Just remember that *you* might be guilty, too—guilty of overthinking things."

"I've faced that accusation before; I dare say I'll face it again." Laidlaw's eyes went to Mason's walking stick. "I'll be hopping along now."

"Do that—and don't ever think about coming back."

Halfway to the house, Laidlaw paused and turned his face towards Mason. "Does that guy still work for you, the one who bites chunks off people's faces for a living?"

"The Snapper, you mean? He got gum disease. They had to whip out all his teeth."

"Ending his business model in the process? I suppose that's the problem when you only have the one skill. A bit like taking Spanner Thomson's spanner away from him. Without it, he's just a guy called Thomson with an empty pocket. Maybe that's how you see Cam Colvin without Bobby Carter. Must be nice to sit here in your garden relaxing and protected while Colvin and Rhodes burn each other's houses down."

"I'd be lying if I said the thought didn't give me a nice warm glow." Mason picked up his paper again and started perusing the racing section. Laidlaw couldn't be sure that he was a betting man necessarily. Maybe he just liked studying the form.

There was no sign of Mason's wife in the house. Laidlaw continued smoking as he walked down the deserted hallway, flicking cigarette ash onto the carpet in his wake.

27

I t was a ten-minute walk to Bobby Carter's street. Laidlaw stopped outside the house opposite and, there being no obvious bell, thumped on the door with his fist. When no one answered, he peered through first the letter box and then the living room window. It was obvious no one was home. He turned his collar up as he prepared for the walk to the nearest bus stop, but then saw a figure emerging from Carter's home. It was Ernie Milligan. Milligan did a double take and a scowl replaced the more relaxed look he'd been sporting. He shoved his hands deep into his coat pockets as he crossed the road and confronted Laidlaw.

"What the hell are you doing here?" he snarled.

"I was just thinking the same thing—keeping the widow to yourself, eh?"

"I was merely providing an update."

"Including Jennifer Love?"

"Monica's got enough on her plate as it is."

"First names now, Ernie? How's everything on the home front—Lucille happy and well?"

Milligan's eyes narrowed. "You're one to talk. I hear you spend more time in hotel beds than your own."

Laidlaw was looking over Milligan's shoulder towards the Carter house. "She's a fine-looking woman, though, and with money coming to her. Can't say I'd blame you for trying, though I doubt you've a cat in hell's chance, not when the competition includes Cam Colvin."

Blood was creeping up Milligan's neck. "I don't want you bothering that family."

"Perish the thought."

"So what *are* you doing here?"

"Just following up the door-to-doors, double-checking what light the neighbours can shed."

"I don't remember that being something I asked for."

"Working on my own initiative, DI Milligan."

"You were at the taxi pound this morning, weren't you? Looks like John Rhodes is preparing for war. Bob Lilley reckons I should try to broker peace."

"Is that right?"

"You don't think I'm up to it?"

"I'm not convinced Gandhi himself would be up to it, but if Bob thinks it's worth a try . . ." Laidlaw gave a shrug.

Milligan was looking past him to where an unmarked Ford Cortina was entering the street, driven by one of the faces from Central. "My lift's here," he stated.

"Room for one in the back?" Laidlaw enquired.

Milligan waited until the car had pulled to a halt before shaking his head with obvious relish. He closed the passenger-side door after him and the car started moving off again, the driver offering an apologetic look in Laidlaw's direction.

"Fuck you too, pal," Laidlaw muttered.

Laidlaw hadn't quite reached the end of the street when he heard a door bang shut behind him. He paused as if to light a cigarette and watched as a young woman approached, chin tucked into the tartan scarf around her neck. She was in her late teens and sported long, straight dark hair, the fringe of which stopped just short of her eyes. He searched for her name: Stella, that was it.

"Stella Carter?" he said as she made to give him a wide berth.

"Which paper are you?"

"I'm police. My colleague DI Milligan just paid you a visit."

"Prove it."

Laidlaw handed her his warrant card. She took her time before returning it.

"He wasn't visiting me," she eventually confided.

"Your mum then. Can I just say how sorry I am about your dad?"

"Stepdad," she corrected him. She had commenced walking again, Laidlaw falling into step beside her.

"Where are you off to?" he asked.

"The shop." After a dozen more steps, she stopped, half turning to stare at him with dark, tired-looking eyes. "What do you want?"

"Twenty Embassy, if you're offering."

She decided to reward him with a fleeting smile. When she recommenced her walk, he stayed with her.

"I didn't know your mum had been married before."

"It didn't last long."

"Long enough to produce you, though."

"I'm the reason for the wedding."

"Some good came of it, then."

"Are you allowed to be chatting me up?"

"Trust me, that's not what I'm doing. Are you in college or anything?"

"Compassionate leave."

Laidlaw nodded his understanding. "What are you studying?"

"Accountancy."

"Your choice or your stepdad's?" When she looked at him, he gave a sympathetic smile. "I went through much the same—literature wasn't going to get me a job, according to my mum and dad. They wanted a doctor, dentist, lawyer, as if the working classes are only allowed higher education as a road towards a trade."

"But you did it anyway? English, I mean?"

"Gave up after a year."

"Drama's what I really wanted to do," she confessed, her tone almost wistful for a moment before she remembered who she was with and the circumstances that had brought them together.

"What was DI Milligan talking to your mum about?" Laidlaw asked into the silence.

"How he's working like a Trojan, not letting up for a second."

"You don't sound convinced."

"He also offered to help move the wall units back now the decorating's finished. Is that part of your normal service?"

"No," Laidlaw conceded.

"No," she agreed. "He just likes my mum—no surprise there."

"I'd say Cam Colvin likes your mum, too."

Stella stared at him and looked suddenly chastened. "Bobby drilled it into us: don't talk to the police. They're not your friends."

"And yet here we are." Laidlaw could see the shop. It was on the next corner, a sandwich board outside tempting customers with offers of cut-price lager and vodka. Time, he knew, was limited. A woman in her seventies had just exited, carrying a string bag containing not much more than a box of loose tea and a bottle of gin.

"Hello there, Stella," she said as she passed them.

"Mrs. Jamieson," Stella replied, the greeting half-hearted at best.

"Cam Colvin does still look in on your mum, though?" Laidlaw asked once they were past.

"He phones mostly. He's arranging the funeral, wants a big show." She paused. "I don't think he was happy when he turned up the same time as Roy."

"Roy?"

"My dad."

"So your mum and him are still close?"

"You ask a lot of questions."

"That's because I'm nosy."

"He takes me out once a fortnight, maybe the pictures or Rothesay or just shopping."

"What does he do for a living?"

"Painter and decorator—thinking of offering him some work?"

"Not a bad idea. My wife's been nagging me for months."

He waited for another smile, but none was being offered.

"You think they might get together again?" he pressed on. "Your mum and dad?"

Stella gave a snort. "Don't think so."

"Stranger things have happened." They had reached the shop's doorway. She pushed her way inside, leaving him standing there. Peering through the glass, he saw her produce a string bag of her own from a pocket, along with a shopping list. Weighing up his options, he turned and headed back the way he'd just come, catching up with Mrs. Jamieson before long, aided by the fact that she seemed to be X-raying every dwelling she passed.

"Carry your bag for you?" he offered.

"No thank you." Her eyes were piercing. "You're the police? I saw you the other day."

Laidlaw nodded. "Not much gets past you," he said. "Must be a shock for the whole street, what happened to Mr. Carter."

"I doubt anybody with eyes and ears was shocked," she snapped back. "The man was a gangster. There was only ever one way that was going to end. You know his boss has been here? Supposedly helping plan the funeral, but I reckon he's digging."

"Digging?"

"Bobby Carter was a lawyer, making him privy to people's secrets."

"We've not had much luck finding evidence of that."

Mrs. Jamieson shrugged her bony shoulders. Laidlaw scratched at his chin. "Did he have much to do with Stella's real father?"

"Wouldn't let him over the threshold. Probably the cause of all the shouting that went on." There was a gleam in the old woman's eye now, and Laidlaw realised she'd been aching to tell someone. He felt like a priest hearing the confession of an over-eager parishioner.

"Shouting, eh?" he prompted. "Husband and wife?"

"Most probably. There's a whole roadway between our houses, you know."

"You were hearing two voices, though?"

"His louder than hers."

"To be clear, this was Bobby and Monica Carter?"

"I couldn't swear it in a court of law."

Perhaps not, Laidlaw thought, but you'd like to try it out for size all the same.

"Arguing about Monica's ex-husband?"

"Some marriages are more volatile than others. They thrive on a bit of argy-bargy."

"You sound as if you speak from experience."

"I threw him out thirty-five years ago." They had reached her gate. Laidlaw undid the latch and pushed it open for her.

"I'm not going to ask the source of discord."

"He just bored me, that's all. Bored me to the back teeth. Being on my own again came as blessed relief." She glanced across the street. "If Monica knows what's good for her, she'll pause for breath before jumping again."

"You're not convinced she will, though?"

"Between her ex and that man Colvin . . ." She shook her head slowly. "Not to mention your own colleague. Men seem

to have no trouble falling for Monica Carter, so be warned."
She took two steps up the path before pausing. "I'd invite you
in for tea, but I'm not feeling particularly sociable."

"Another time, then." Laidlaw gave a little bow of the head.
He knew she had a prior appointment with the bottle of gin in
her bag. The memory of its predecessor had been lingering on
her breath as they'd talked.

28

W hat are you doing here?" Bob Lilley asked, a look of disbelief on his face.

"I thought I worked here," Laidlaw answered.

"I was beginning to have my doubts." Lilley slung his jacket over the back of his chair and approached Laidlaw's desk. "Seen this?" He held out the front page of the *Herald*. There was a photo of a DCI they both knew. He was crouched by the incinerator in the HQ's boiler room, disposing of a large haul of cannabis.

"Somebody's hopes and dreams going up in smoke," Laidlaw commented. He had tipped his chair back, his feet on his desk. Paperwork was piled on his lap, discarded sheets strewn across the floor beneath him. Lilley picked one up and studied it.

"The victim's background?"

"Background and personal life, Bob." Laidlaw took the biro from between his teeth and underlined a couple of typed sentences. "Why did we give it such short shrift?"

"I'm not convinced *we* did, though you might have."

Laidlaw ignored the dig. "Monica was married before, to a guy called Roy Chambers. He's a decorator. Stella's his daughter."

"I know."

"Hardly a year after she split with Chambers, she was with Bobby Carter. Stella would have been three or thereabouts. Then along come two half-brothers for her, Peter and Christopher."

"Your point being?"

"Roy kept in touch, but he was *persona non grata* as far as Bobby Carter was concerned." Laidlaw had picked up a photograph of Monica. "She's handsome rather than beautiful, that's my opinion anyway. But she's wearing well. She's four years older than Bobby—did you know that?"

"The allure of the older woman." Lilley had rested his backside against the corner of Laidlaw's desk.

"Where have you been anyway?"

"Various doorsteps."

"Did they get you anywhere?"

"What do you think? So why the sudden interest in the family? You thinking we need to talk to this Roy character?"

"Bobby and Monica had arguments—a neighbour heard them. Though it could have been Bobby and Stella, or maybe one of the brothers and Stella . . ."

"Or one of the boys and his mum," Lilley added. "I had a few shouting matches with mine when they were in their teens."

"What about?"

"Just the usual—if they'd been drinking or stayed out past curfew. Those joys are doubtless waiting for you in your future."

"My kids are never growing up, not if I've got anything to do with it."

"Doesn't work that way, though."

"Let's see. Meantime, this Roy Chambers doesn't seem to have a record. I've not got a photo of him yet, either." Another sheet of paper dropped to the floor from Laidlaw's hand. Lilley noted something missing from the desk.

"What happened to your books?"

Laidlaw reached into a drawer, pulling one of them out. Its cover had been vandalised with a cock and balls.

"Nice," Lilley commented.

"I've drawn up a list of suspects." Laidlaw's glare took in the whole room.

"Am I on it?" Lilley watched Laidlaw shake his head, toss the book back into the drawer and slam it shut. "I meant to ask, what did you get out of Matt Mason?"

"The verbal equivalent of a defaced book jacket."

"One of these days, sticking your head in every lion's mouth you pass is going to end badly."

"You're probably right. Winners and losers, though, Bob— who stands to gain from Carter's demise? Long term as well as short term."

Lilley puckered his mouth in thought. "Could this guy Chambers want back in his ex-wife's knickers?"

"Probably black, silky and lacy. Milligan was sniffing around again, too."

"You've been out to the house, then?"

"Happened to be passing through after my chat with Mason."

"To go back to your earlier question—Mason definitely stands to gain from any feud between Cam Colvin and John Rhodes."

Laidlaw nodded. "Which doesn't necessarily mean he's our man. There's a goon posted at his front door with what looks remarkably like a gun tucked inside his jacket. What does that tell you?"

"He's worried that either Rhodes or Colvin will put two and two together and come looking for him?"

"Or else he's jittery because he has no bloody idea who's behind any of it."

"Reading between the lines, though, sounds to me like you think *you're* narrowing it down."

"I think I am, too. Problem is, it's almost too narrow for my liking."

"What does that mean?"

Laidlaw shook his head. "I need to get back to this lot," he said, gesturing towards the case notes.

"Pint later, then?"

"I could be tempted by some thinking juice."

"At which point I'll become privy to that thinking?"

Laidlaw looked up at him. "You're the second person to use that word in as many hours."

"Privy?"

"I thought you'd be like me, Bob, thinking it only meant shitehouse."

Lilley looked at the mess of papers on the floor. "Don't be surprised if Ernie Milligan accuses you of living in one when he gets back."

He waited for a response, but Laidlaw's attention was on the latest batch of notes, so he left him to it.

29

A rchie Love was always the last to leave the park. There was a single-storey prefab building that the players used as a changing room. No showers, just a single WC, benches ranged down two walls and another wall of lockers. He liked to linger once everyone else had gone, allowing him to think back to his early days as a player. In the junior leagues, he'd got used to being the star of the show, the one the opposition had in their sights for a studs-up sliding tackle or a sly dig in the kidneys. Later, having signed as a professional, he discovered he was no longer the best. The advice he'd been given was to stick in and he might get there. He body-swerved alcohol and too many late nights, was out exercising from first light, and never shirked a practice session or tactics talk. He knew his playing career could be ended at any moment by injury or a clash of personalities. Even if he stayed lucky, he had between five and ten good years in him. Management was his goal, but he'd never been offered the chance. Nowadays he told the best of his young players that they had to think long term, had to put money aside for the rainy days ahead, and whatever they did, they should on no account open a pub. There were only two ways that ever ended: penury or alcoholism.

He didn't feel particularly bad about the ones he approached to sway a result. He always did his research. Speaking of which, the bugger was ten minutes late. But then the door creaked and Love adjusted his posture accordingly.

The man who walked in looked prosperous enough and fit enough. The coat he wore was new, and there was a chunky gold ID bracelet dangling from one wrist. There was a bit of a glow still left around him, telling those he met that he had a reputation. But Archie Love knew that Geoff Inglis had already passed his personal high-water mark; now he was in his thickening thirties. He might keep splashing, but he was in a pool growing shallower all the time.

"Mr. Love," Inglis said by way of greeting.

"I always liked that about you, Geoff," Love replied with an indulgent smile. "You show respect."

Inglis shrugged and began looking around the changing room. He wasn't tall, but in his day he had commanded the midfield with a no-nonsense pugnacity. "You taught me a hell of a lot, back in the day."

"All started here, didn't it, Geoff? Not *here* exactly, but a set-up just like it, muddy pitch outside and makeshift goal-posts. But you applied yourself and you went places. I was always proud of you." Love glanced at the mirror opposite, checking he looked sincere.

"Never quite got that Scotland cap, though."

"Not for want of trying."

"So what is it I can do for you, Mr. Love?"

Love gave an extended sigh. "I hate the way they're treating you, Geoff. Focusing on the younger faces, the fresher legs. We both know you're on the transfer list. By the summer, you could even be on a free."

Geoff Inglis pulled back his shoulders. "Might not come to that."

"You're not daft, Geoff. It will *exactly* come to that. Loyalty counts for nothing these days. You've given your life to this game and you end up overlooked and unrewarded. I *hate* to see that happen, especially to a decent individual like yourself. We both know there's a slow descent coming—lower leagues, maybe semi-pro, and then you're on your arse." Love paused, locking eyes with Inglis. He had the man's attention. It was time for a change of pace. He allowed his face to droop a little. "I had a son, did you know that?

"I don't think I did."

"He died young, far too young. He had a bit of talent, maybe could have made it. All of you boys, the ones I helped climb the ladder . . . well, it's almost embarrassing to say it out loud . . ."

"What is?"

Love's eyes were growing liquid. "You're all like sons to me." He inhaled and exhaled. "Which is why I try to help when I can."

"Help how?"

"Something to cushion your backside as you slide down that hill."

Inglis's brow had furrowed. "I'm not sure I follow."

Then you dress sharper than you think . . .

Love wafted a hand in front of him as if to dismiss the idea. "Look, it's just something that I can sometimes make happen. But I'd have to be sure you really wanted it. Will you do me a huge favour? Go away and mull it over. Think about your future and what you'd like to see there. I've got some contacts and they can maybe help those dreams become reality."

"I don't know exactly what it is you're asking of me."

Love could see that right enough, but nor did he want to spell it out. Inglis had to join the dots for himself. The less Love said, the less there was to incriminate him. If Geoff Inglis did work it out, he would come back and ask the question, and Archie Love would answer "maybe." Then Inglis would ask: how much money are we talking about? But Love would be coy about that, too, while emphasising that his friends could prove very helpful to Geoff in the future. They would be in his debt and they wouldn't forget. They were people to whom loyalty was still a point of principle.

Not that Matt Mason ever *would* lend that hand, or [ ]
thing else come to that.

But if Inglis was still unsure, Love might add that one [ ]
slip-up in a game was hardly going to prove a memorable [ ]
ish on a long and distinguished career. Teams would sti[ ]
interested. A move into management was always a possibil[ ]

For now, though, he had planted the seed, just as he pla[ ]
his hand in front of him for the younger man to shake, [ ]
looking bemused but starting the process of working th[ ]
out.

"You've come a long way, son," Love said in closing. "[ ]
deserve a lot more than they're willing to give you. Take it f[ ]
one who knows, a pocket filled with banknotes beats a d[ ]
cap in a trophy cabinet any day of the week." He placed a h[ ]
on Inglis's back, steering him towards the door.

Once that was done, he turned to face the empty room o[ ]
more. There were dollops of mud on the linoleum-tiled fl[ ]
blades of grass embedded in them. A cleaner would be [ ]
tomorrow to deal with it. He had found himself itching to [ ]
this evening for some reason, had actually almost sprinted o[ ]
the pitch. Fear and common sense had eventually prevail[ ]
His power came from his past achievements. In the you[ ]
men's minds he was a success story. If he took to the field a[ ]
was immediately dispossessed, or made a series of poor pass[ ]
or committed an error leading to a goal, that power would [ ]
lost irreparably. Instead, he had dug his bunched fists deep[ ]
into his tracksuit pockets and bellowed instructions all t[ ]
louder.

Now he lowered himself onto one of the benches, elbo[ ]
on his knees and head in his hands. Inglis would either take t[ ]
bait or he wouldn't. Plenty more fish in that particular se[ ]
Love knew he was delaying the moment when he would ha[ ]
to return home, where his wife and daughter waited, unite[ ]
against him. Chick McAllister *and* Bobby Carter? He ha[ ]

flung up his hands at the horror of it, while Jennifer sat there reduced to a sulky adolescent, arms folded and head bowed.

"It's her life," his wife had argued, standing guard beside the sofa their daughter sat on as if to ward off a physical assault.

"I'm her dad! It should have been *you* that told me, not the bloody polis!"

"What's done is done, Archie. Jennifer's learned her lesson."

Had she, though? He'd asked her that very question, causing her to storm out of the room, only to return a few seconds later.

"I never even let him shag me!" she had screamed, before making a second exit. He had glared at his wife.

"She did sleep with McAllister, then? I dare say you knew all about that, too?"

Could anyone blame him for wanting to stay a few extra minutes in the dressing room? He could feel the padlock in his pocket, next to his referee's whistle and stopwatch. Once he'd locked up, there would be no alternative but to head home for another wordless evening meal, followed by a few generous whiskies and a silenced bed.

When the door creaked open, he reckoned at first that Geoff Inglis's brain cells had kicked in, driving him to a speedy decision. But the two men who entered were strangers to him and didn't look in the least bit friendly.

"Archie Love?" one of them asked.

"Who wants to know?"

The questioner towered over Love, staring down at him.

"You're Archie Love," he said with a humourless smile. "Your photo was in the paper when you played for Rangers."

"Your memory's better than your attitude, son." Love started to get to his feet, but the man pushed down on one of his shoulders, hinting that he should stay seated. Love noted that the other man—stockier, one hand tucked inside his coat—was toeing open some of the empty lockers.

"Nothing worth nicking here," Love informed him.

"Got a few questions for you about your daughter," the first man stated. "The one who strips for a living."

"She dances, that's all." Love bristled.

"In a skirt short enough to get every crotch in the place bulging."

Love sprang to his feet, shoving aside the hand that had been holding him down. That same hand shot forward into his gut, winding him, nearly causing his knees to buckle.

"You're not being very clever," the man said. "Matt Mason doesn't like a stupid lackey. They tend to end up retired with no pension."

"I don't work for Matt Mason," Love said, wincing with the effort.

"You do, though. It was the first thing people told us when we started asking about you. So if you were reckoning it a well-kept secret, you might want to think again."

Love saw that the other man had grown bored of checking the lockers and had taken a couple of steps closer to the bench. His hand was no longer inside his coat. Instead, it was clutching a new-looking industrial-sized spanner. Love knew what that meant, knew that a man going by the name of Spanner Thomson was muscle for Cam Colvin.

"I had nothing to do with whatever happened to Bobby Carter," he blurted out.

"Your daughter was seeing a married man, Archie. That can't have appealed to you, surely."

"Which is why she kept it from me—her and her mum both."

"How about Chick McAllister? Do you still see him around the place?"

"No."

"You sure about that?"

Love had opened his mouth to speak when the spanner

caught him square on his forehead. This time he did drop to his knees, raising one arm over his skull to ward off further blows. The man who wasn't Thomson leaned down and hooked a finger under his chin, angling his face upwards.

"Does Matt Mason have designs on our boss's territory?"

"How the hell would I know?"

"Because from what I hear, some people still look up to you—fuck knows why, but they do. And to impress you, they might want to tell you things."

"I don't know the first thing about Matt Mason's business."

"So what did you say to the police when they spoke to you?"

Love bit down hard on his bottom lip. Someone had grassed on him—had to be one of his two assistants. They knew cops when they saw them. Probably knew about Jennifer and Carter, too. But they had kept that to themselves, teasing him behind his back, smirking and laughing.

"I didn't know anything about my daughter and Carter until he told me."

"He being . . . ?"

"Laidlaw, he said his name was. Big guy, smoker, lot going on behind the eyes."

"We know Laidlaw. Why was he talking to you?"

The spanner's cold steel had come to rest against Love's left cheek, clamouring for his attention.

"Because of Jennifer. He seemed interested in Chick McAllister, too."

"You know McAllister works for John Rhodes?" The man watched as Archie Love gave a nod. "You knew that back when they were winching?" Another nod. "What did Matt Mason have to say about that?"

"Family was family, he said, just so long as it didn't interfere with business."

"Well, Bobby Carter was *our* business partner, but he was practically family, too. So we're taking his death a bit more personally, if you understand what I mean. If we have a wee word with your daughter, what will she tell us?"

"There's no need for that."

"What will she tell us?" the man persisted.

"There's nothing to tell. Bobby Carter liked her well enough, but a friend was all he was going to get and that wasn't satisfactory. They split up without really falling out. Next night, she saw him out on the pull again, as if she hadn't meant much of anything to him at all."

"Jenni told you that?"

"Her mum did, eventually."

"The night she saw him, did he have anyone in his sights in particular?"

"I can ask her."

"But will you ask her properly, so we don't have to?"

Love's nod this time was more resolute.

"What do you think, Spanner? You reckon Mr. Love here knows that if we're unhappy with the results, we'll be back wearing our pissed-off faces?"

In answer, the spanner rose up, coming down hard on Love's shoulder blade. He gasped in pain. The finger had been removed from his chin, and he dropped to all fours.

"Fair warning," he heard the first man say.

Blinking his eyes clear of tears, he saw the two pairs of well-shod feet moving towards the door. It slammed shut after them. He hauled himself back onto the bench, breathing hard, his whole body sparking from the encounter. There were bits of mud and grass between his fingers. Only an hour before, he'd felt in charge, issuing orders and advice, a king of sorts.

He felt so much less than that now. And for the first time since his footballing career had ended in ignominy, Archie Love allowed himself to weep.

30

T hat evening, Spanner Thomson and Mickey Ballater hit a few pubs. To start with, Panda and Dod were with them and all four pretended they were digging up information. They even pulled a few known faces to one side and asked some questions. What was the word on Bobby Carter's demise? Any whispers about John Rhodes or Matt Mason? Eventually, Panda and Dod peeled off, leaving Spanner and Mickey at a corner table—vacated for their benefit—in yet another nondescript howff peopled by regulars who knew better than to bother them. Spanner Thomson drank bottled beer—not trusting the stuff out of the tap, explaining to Mickey that bottles were infinitely more hygienic, especially if you didn't then use a glass. Ballater himself was on the vodka, diluted with sweetened orange juice.

"Let's skedaddle," Ballater eventually said. "This place is boring the tits off me."

"The casino?"

"I was thinking Whiskies. Eye up a few of the birds."

"Would those birds include Jenni Love?"

"You know me too well, Spanner." A grin spread across Mickey Ballater's face.

It was mild enough for them to walk. A drunk staggered into them almost as soon as they were on the pavement. Thomson gave the man a shove hard enough to send him flying. A couple of other pedestrians looked ready to step in until they saw who they'd be dealing with. Thomson and Ballater felt that they fully owned these streets as they strode through them. Clusters of hardened men parted like the Red Sea, so they had no need to steer anything but a straight course. A shame, actually. Ever since he'd watched the spanner connect with Love's forehead, Mickey Ballater had been wanting to enact some violent action of his own.

"One thing's for sure," Spanner commented as they walked along. "The boss isn't going to be happy if things keep going like this."

"We could always gift-wrap him someone like Archie Love. Bury him deep and tell Cam he confessed."

"Cam wants to hear it from the culprit's own lips, remember."

Ballater grunted. He had his eye on an approaching teenager, dressed in head-to-toe denim, Rangers scarf tight around his neck. The boy was smart enough to cross the street, even at the risk of a passing taxi clipping him. The taxi sounded its horn and the teenager flicked the Vs.

"I love this place," Ballater said.

"Odds are shifting towards Matt Mason," Thomson went on, not about to have his train of thought derailed. "Start a war, then sit back and watch."

"Wasn't it you who said Mason's happy enough the way things are?"

"That was Panda."

"I got the feeling you agreed with him."

"Maybe I'm changing my mind."

"Since your wee chat with John Rhodes?"

Thomson fixed his companion with a look. "I've already explained about that."

"What about the boss's theory, then—Bobby had turned detective to see if Mason had anyone from our side on his pay-roll?"

Thomson shook his head. "That would be a nice excuse for Bobby to go and meet a few people."

"You think he was about to jump ship? Cam wouldn't have let that happen."

"Exactly."

It was Ballater's turn to look at Thomson. "There's no way Cam did this. It's too messy."

"But he could have let it be known he wouldn't be too bothered if it transpired."

"So why not say something to us?"

They were passing a knot of middle-aged men, caps fixed tightly to heads, collars up. There were greetings, the intoning of "Mickey" and "Spanner." It felt almost liturgical, these men hungry for a blessing, receiving at best a nodded acknowledgement of their existence.

Once they were past, Thomson spoke in an undertone. "John Rhodes told me Bobby Carter was thinking of setting up a rival firm."

"That's just Rhodes talking, though."

"Is it?"

"Did you mention this to Cam?"

Thomson nodded. "He as good as told me to back off."

"You think he already knew? Justice would have been swift if he did."

"Maybe."

"He's always thought you were jealous of Bobby." Ballater was thoughtful for as long as it took him to hawk up some spit and lob it towards the roadway. A woman in horn-rimmed glasses and headscarf gave him a look, receiving a leer in reply. "He's been up to high doh since Bobby's death," he told Thomson. "You telling me that's for show?"

"We're all of us good at putting on a show, Mickey." Thomson was looking at his companion again.

"I don't get your meaning, Spanner," Ballater said darkly.

"Bobby's summer party. You and Monica round the side of the house by the garage."

Mickey Ballater stopped in his tracks. "You saw that?"

"I saw." The two men were facing one another now. Thomson had a hand shoved deep in one of his coat pockets, having brought his unfinished bottle of McEwan's with him. Only an inch left in it, if that, but Spanner Thomson was not a man to waste anything.

Ballater forced a smile. "And you kept it to yourself?"

"So far."

"Maybe you were out looking for her, eh? Fancied your own chances?" Ballater gave his companion a chance to speak, but Spanner stayed quiet, so he offered a shrug. "It was nothing." He started walking again, Thomson following suit.

"It looked like something."

"I admit I tried it on, but she wasn't having it."

"Might be a different story with Bobby out of the picture." Ballater shook his head slowly. His face would look calm enough to any onlooker, but his voice was a meeting of fire and ice. "You're out of order, Spanner. *You're* the one Cam's bothered about, not me."

"Cam knows he can trust me."

"Is that right, aye?"

"Did he tell you different? When you went back to see him yesterday?" Thomson had grabbed Ballater by the sleeve of his jacket, the two men stopping again, the air around them crackling.

"It was a private chat, Spanner. Best ask Cam if you want to know."

"Maybe I'll do that, and this time I won't forget to mention you and Bobby Carter's missus. The feelings he has for her, he's going to want to know."

They stared at one another like boxers sizing one another up before the bell rang and hostilities commenced. A reveller across the street began belting out a rough but impassioned version of "My Way." Ballater's eyes moved towards the man then back again to Spanner Thomson. The smile he gave could almost have been described as coy.

"You're right about Cam. He's not sure who to trust right now, and you allowing Rhodes into your car set off all his alarm bells. He wants me keeping an eye on you. I'm happy to tell him he's got nothing to worry about."

"In which case that summer party might slip my memory."

"Say things do escalate, though—won't be long before Rhodes's team come for one of us. If that happens, we have to hit them back hard. Things are going to get worse before they get better."

"This is Glasgow, Mickey. Things have been getting worse since the end of the tobacco barons."

"What I'm saying is, we should make provision. If Cam falls . . . perish the thought, but if he does, we need a backup plan."

"We as in you and me, or are you including Panda and Dod in this?"

Ballater shrugged. "Have you got a preference? Because right now this is just you and me talking." He looked to left and right. The busy city-centre street was giving them the widest of berths.

"You wouldn't sell Cam out?" Thomson enquired.

"Under no circumstances, but that doesn't mean he won't be *forced* out at some point, after which our health and general well-being might not be so secure. You've got John Rhodes rooting for you, Spanner, but who have I got?"

"Rhodes only wants me because he thinks I lead him straight to Cam. That's why he was waiting for me. But he wouldn't have done that if someone hadn't planted the knife in my neighbourhood. I'm the careful sort, Mickey, won't even have a phone in the house. Not too many people know where I live. I doubt even John Rhodes knew until the cops came to see me."

"What are you saying?"

"I'm saying I don't trust any of you—not you, not Panda, not Dod."

"You still trust your old pal Cam, though, even though he wants me reporting back everything you're up to?"

Spanner Thomson's face almost collapsed. It was as if every memory from childhood onwards was crashing down on him, like a roof whose supporting beams had been hollowed out until they could no longer bear the load.

"Cam's covering all the eventualities, that's all," he eventually muttered.

"And that's what I'm talking about, Spanner." Ballater leaned in towards him. "We're all just trying to survive, aren't we? If we can dodge a few tripwires along the way, so much the better."

"And in the meantime, you fancy yourself for that empty chair next to Cam?"

Ballater shook his head emphatically. "You're his oldest friend, Spanner. That position's yours by rights. I can't believe Cam's not already installed you. Now are we going to stand here all night, because if we are, I might get somebody to fetch us a few drinks."

Thomson brought his bottle out and shook it. "Got mine right here." He lifted it to his lips and drained it. Ballater knew this was the moment. He could shove with the heel of his hand, sending the neck of the bottle past Thomson's splintering teeth and deep down his throat. Instead of which, he gave a convincing-sounding laugh.

"You're some boy, Spanner. Drinks are on me when we get to Whiskies."

"Price they charge in there, I just might take you up on that."

The two men started walking, their destination not far now. Thomson tossed the empty bottle over one shoulder. It shattered as it hit the pavement. Neither man so much as turned their head.

Eyes front.

Never look back.

Quiet all the way to the club, each digging deep into his own thoughts and schemes.

31

S panner had the taxi drop him off outside Springburn Park. It was well enough lit and the teenagers hanging around there knew better than to try messing with him. He found himself standing next to the taped-off section where the knife had been planted. It wasn't near any stretch of roadway or pavement. You had to walk towards the centre of the park to reach it. He wondered if whoever had left the knife there had been crossing the park, maybe intending to deposit it closer to the house. But that would have been too obvious a set-up. Further away was better; further away told the story of a killer who finds panic setting in as they return to their senses. So they toss the weapon, suddenly keen to get rid of it.

Putting Spanner Thomson firmly in the frame.

He had told Ballater that he doubted John Rhodes had known his address until the police had come to call. But Mickey Ballater himself knew it, as did Panda Paterson and Dod Menzies. Several times he'd treated them to drinks in the back garden, Mary handing round meat-paste sandwiches from which she'd removed the crusts. Cam had been there too, of course, taking him aside to try to persuade him to buy somewhere grander in a nicer part of town.

"Otherwise people will start saying I'm not looking after you—and we both know that's not true."

But Spanner had grown up on the streets of Balornock. He felt safe there. And with no kids to show for his fourteen years of marriage, why would he need anything bigger? The money he brought home went to Mary, and she squirrelled anything they didn't need into a building society account. There was some cash she didn't know about, of course, set aside by Spanner in case he ever needed a quick getaway. He'd actually thought about it after that visit to Central Division. Two things stopped him. One was that it would make him look all the guiltier in everyone's eyes, Cam included. The other was that he was raging inside, with a need to find out who was stitching him up.

Someone who knew that empty chair was his by right.

Someone who knew his address.

Someone very like Mickey Ballater.

He paused at the gate leading to his house, then continued past to the nearest phone box. It smelled of pee inside, but at least there was a dial tone when he lifted the receiver, having first pulled his sleeve down to cover his hand, wary of germs. He dialled the number and pushed home a coin when Cam Colvin answered.

"It's me, Cam."

"I know that, Spanner—who else calls me from a public phone? What's on your mind at this time of night?"

Thomson could hear soft music playing in the background, either a record or the radio.

"Sorry to be interrupting your evening."

"I assume there's news that can't wait."

He exhaled noisily. "It's maybe nothing, but I've been talking to Mickey."

"Oh aye?"

"I'm not sure you can trust him. I mean, you maybe think you can't trust me either—he told me you'd ordered him to keep an eye on me . . ."

"Did he now?"

"But swear to God I'm not the one you should be watching," Thomson blurted out. "It won't take much for him to jump ship—always supposing he can't have your job. That's what I think he's interested in; not Bobby's chair but yours, and I doubt he's too bothered how that comes about." He paused. "And there's another thing—I saw him with Monica, at that party of Bobby's back in the summer. They were having a snog."

There was a lengthening silence on the line.

"Are you sure about that, Spanner?" Colvin eventually asked, sounding as if he were working hard to keep his emotions in check.

You really think you're in with a chance there, don't you, Cam, now that Bobby's out of the picture? Could that really be why he had to be got rid of?

"I know what I saw," Thomson heard himself say. It was as if he were floating in the space between the top of his head and the roof of the phone box, watching someone else inhabit his body. "Mickey says he tried his luck but she was having none of it. That's not how it looked to me, though."

"You think they were seeing one another behind Bobby's back?"

"Honest answer is, I don't know. Maybe you should ask him."

"I might have to do that, Spanner."

Thomson opened his mouth to say something further, but the line had already gone dead.

As he navigated the short distance back to his home, his bed and his waiting wife, he felt a sadness wrapping itself around him. His universe had been both comprehensible and robust until Bobby Carter's death. Now it was anything but. The feeling of unease was both unusual and unwelcome. Something would have to be done about it.

Something *would* be done about it.

DAY SIX

32

Roy Chambers' decorating business had its headquarters in Partick. The mid-morning air was chill, Laidlaw's breath appearing before him in little puffs as he strode along the pavement. A double-decker wheezed past, its windows misted over. None of the passengers had bothered wiping them clean, there being nothing outside worthy of their attention. RC Interiors boasted a swish name but comprised a single window containing a display of wallpaper sample books and two rolls of woodchip, and a door whose glazed upper half was stickered with adverts for paint manufacturers. There was also a sign. The sign read CLOSED. Laidlaw tried the door anyway. It was locked. He gave it a thump and a kick. Eventually a young woman appeared from the back of the shop. She peered at him and kept the chain on when she unlocked the door. He pressed his warrant card into the gap.

"I'm looking to speak to Roy," he said.

She closed the door long enough to remove the chain, then opened it again.

"Can't be too careful," she said.

"Especially when there's so much treasure within," Laidlaw agreed.

"Roy's out on a job. I run the office for him."

Laidlaw nodded his understanding. She was in her late teens, stout but self-aware and comfortable with the fact. She was done up to the nines, as though at any moment she might have to present herself as the public face of RC Interiors. She had been raised to dress well, give a good account of herself and take no nonsense.

"Are you family?"

"I'm his niece. What has he done wrong?"

"I thought you'd never ask."

"I didn't ask because I can't imagine him ever doing something that would bring the likes of you running."

"Yet here the likes of me stands, unless you're going to invite me in."

"What's the point? I've already told you he's not here."

"Then give me an address and I'll be on my way."

"Is it to do with what happened to Bobby Carter?"

"What makes you say that?"

She smiled to herself. "It is, though, isn't it? Because Roy used to be married to Monica. I told him the police would be interested."

"Clever girl. Now about that address . . ."

"He wouldn't hurt a fly."

"I'll take your word for it."

"You won't, though, will you? You still need to talk to him?"

"Unfortunately that's the way things work."

"I've applied to join the police, you know."

"Want me to put in a word?"

"That's not how it's done. I'm not daft."

"I'm well aware of that, even from this brief exchange."

They stood in silence for a moment as she gnawed at her bottom lip. Then she spun round and headed to her office, sidestepping pots of paint and bottles of turps. Laidlaw followed her.

The shop's interior had an inviting aroma. He wondered if it was coming from the wallpaper samples piled up on the room's only table. Radio 1 was playing, the transistor perched on a shelf above the office desk. This back room was a cramped space, with a door off that gave a view of a toilet pan and washbasin.

Anyone breaking in through the narrow and barred window to the rear would have to manoeuvre their way past the variety of ladders stored there. The girl was leafing through an old-fashioned ledger. Finding the address, she snatched up a pencil and jotted it down on a notepad for him, tearing off the sheet once finished and handing it over with a flourish.

"I never caught your name," he said.

"Janine."

"Any other career plans apart from the police, Janine?"

"Art school maybe. I've done a bit of modelling and it looks interesting."

"Strikes me, whatever you decide to do with your life you'll make a go of it. Is Roy a one-man outfit?"

"It's a big job, this." She nodded towards the scrap of paper. "He'll have Gordy with him." She unwrapped a stick of chewing gum and popped it between her lips. "Is being a detective as exciting as it looks on TV?"

"Never a dull moment."

"You're saying that tongue in cheek, aren't you?"

"I'm saying I wish I was still an artist's model. Thanks for the address, Janine."

Kelvingrove wasn't far from Partick if you were talking in terms of miles, yards and feet. On the other hand, it was an entirely separate world of grand nineteenth-century sandstone terraces plus the elegant park and busy museum. Laidlaw had last visited the museum with his kids, wondering why they hadn't been half as keen on the Dali Christ as he was. The house outside which Roy Chambers' van was parked had obviously already had a lot of work done to its facade. Laidlaw could tell where new stonework had replaced old. The front door gaped, but before heading inside, he stopped at the van, whose rear door was open, a young man seated there next to a flask of tea.

"You must be Gordy," he said. The lad squinted up at him. He wore bespattered white overalls with a pale blue T-shirt beneath and didn't seem to be feeling the cold. "I take it Roy's indoors?"

Gordy merely shrugged and began rolling a cigarette.

"How much time did you do?" Laidlaw enquired.

"Knew straight off you were polis."

"Same as I knew you've seen the inside of Barlinnie. A wee thin roll-up like that, not wanting to use too much precious tobacco, is a classic tell. Then there are the tattoos."

Gordy examined his arms.

"Somewhere between home-made and professional," Laidlaw went on. "I've seen more than a few in my time."

"I was a daft laddie," Gordy commented. "That's all it boils down to."

"Picked up a trade while you were inside, though. That speaks of something. How long have you known Roy?"

"Go ask him." Gordy poured the dregs of his tea onto the ground so that splashes hit Laidlaw's shoes.

"I intend to. How long have you been out?"

"I'm done talking." The young man rose to his feet, closed and locked the van doors and headed up the steps to the imposing front door. It had been given several coats of black gloss paint and the Greek-style columns flanking it were both recent replacements. Beyond lay a black and white tiled floor, several doors off, and a sweeping staircase. Scaffolding had been erected in the middle of the floor, dust sheets spread beneath it. The stairs were similarly protected.

"We've got company!" Gordy yelled, his voice echoing in the vast space. A head appeared from one of the rooms on the first floor, peering over the stair rail.

"The name's Detective Constable Laidlaw," Laidlaw explained. "Wondered if I could have a word with you."

"Did Janine give you the address?" The man was already

descending the stairs. He was dressed in identical overalls to his junior partner, though the T-shirt beneath was black and dotted with smears of paint. The freckles on Roy Chambers' face turned out, on closer inspection, to be spots of paint too. He wore socks with no shoes and Laidlaw noticed that, now he was indoors, Gordy had removed his own Doc Martens.

"She did."

"She's thinking of applying to the police."

"She mentioned it," Laidlaw said, while behind him Gordy gave a snort of derision.

Chambers had taken a rag from his pocket and was wiping his hands. His hair was short and russet-coloured, his frame tall and wiry. Laidlaw judged him to be a few years younger than his ex-wife; more Bobby Carter's age, in fact.

"I was talking to your daughter," Laidlaw went on, "and she said you'd been to the house. Since Mr. Carter died, I mean."

Chambers gave a thoughtful nod. "Cam Colvin was there, so I never got past the threshold, much like old times."

"Stella told me Carter didn't take to you."

"Understandable, I suppose. That what this is about—I'm supposed to have done him in?"

"Did you?"

"No."

"Ever think about doing it?"

Chambers shrugged and stuffed the rag back into his pocket. "Monica and me still got on. Then there was Stella to consider. I wanted to be part of her life. At one point, she was thinking of moving into my flat."

"That didn't happen, though?"

"I think Carter put his foot down. And just when Monica's shot of him, along comes Cam bloody Colvin."

"Colvin and Carter were close; it's only natural he'd want to do right by the family."

"It's not the family he wants, though, is it? It's Monica."

"Now that Carter presents no barrier, do you think Stella might come live with you?"

"That's one of the things I wanted to discuss with her and her mum."

"But Colvin had other ideas?"

"You don't want to get on the wrong side of Cam Colvin," Gordy commented. Laidlaw got the feeling he'd given the warning to his employer more than once in the past.

Laidlaw made show of studying the pristine surroundings. "Whoever owns this place must have a few bob."

"Some professor at the uni," Chambers said, "yet teachers are always moaning about their pay. We've got until Friday to finish it." He glanced towards Gordy. "Few late nights still ahead."

"Maybe once you finish, you can take over the decorating at your ex-wife's house," Laidlaw said, readying to leave. "Now that Bobby Carter's not around to say no."

Chambers' eyebrows rose almost to his hairline. "She's redecorating already? It was only done a couple of months back." He shook his head sorrowfully. "Mind you, I told her the paint choices were all wrong, and the firm Carter hired were absolute bloody cowboys . . ."

33

L aidlaw's head was spinning as he left Kelvingrove on foot. Nearing a bus stop as a double-decker paused to let off a passenger, he climbed aboard and headed upstairs. The seats near the front were taken, but that didn't bother him. It wasn't the view he was interested in; he just needed to think. He dug out a few coins at the conductor's approach and gripped the resultant ticket, managing to light a cigarette at the same time, sucking the smoke deep. Before he knew it, it had been reduced to a stub. He crushed it under his heel and lit another. Outside he saw a group of young men wearing football scarves. Was today Saturday? Who was playing? He had no idea. Time had ceased to mean anything. He had listened to murderers tell him during their confession that time stopped at the exact moment their victim stopped breathing, while the assailant felt as if they had departed their corporeal form and were hovering overhead, looking down on the frozen tableau. Seconds became hours, or else hours became compressed into mere blinks of the eye. No, they couldn't remember the moments leading up to the crime, or telephoning 999, or washing the blood from their hands. *Was* it a Saturday, though? He hoped to hell the Old Firm weren't playing. Those were the worst, the losing fans filled with rage as they headed home to families who held their collective breath for fear of reprisal.

Domestics: that was the term that was starting to be used. Violence carried out against you in the one place that was meant to be your refuge, your domain, your nest. Wives would go out shopping or to work on a Monday morning with a thick layer of make-up covering the damage. They would look haunted and broken, shunning eye contact, answers prepared for the questions they'd be asked by neighbours, friends, office or factory colleagues.

It was a wonder more didn't do something about it.

Some did, though. Some did.

As Laidlaw became aware of the route the bus was taking, he realised he was nearing Central Division's orbit. He got off at the next stop, lingering in the graffitied shelter as he finished the cigarette—it was either his second or third of the trip. He paced as he smoked. *Redecorating already . . . absolute bloody cowboys.*

"Stupid, Jack, stupid, stupid," he muttered to himself, beyond caring if anyone thought him odd. He *was* odd—odd and stupid and sometimes wrong. But not this time. Because it made sense. For the first time since Bobby Carter's death, everything made perfect sense.

He walked the rest of the short distance to the HQ building blinded to everything except the simplicity of what had occurred. He went straight to the crime squad office and looked around, ignoring Bob Lilley as he sought the one person he needed. Lilley, however, was not to be thwarted. He approached with what could have passed for a penitent look.

"I'm under orders to fix a return date for a meal." He broke off as he noticed Laidlaw's agitation. "What's happened?"

"Everything and nothing."

"More wisdom from your philosophers?" Lilley nodded towards Laidlaw's desk drawer. Laidlaw stared at him.

"Know why they're there, Bob, those books?" The words tumbled from his mouth. "It's because in a room full of detectives, they'll be seen as clues to my character, and while everyone's busy trying to decipher their role and meaning, I can get some work done unhindered." He had a fevered look to him as he stared at his colleague. "I think we've been following a string of MacGuffins that's only got longer as this case has unfolded."

"Who the hell's MacGuffin?"

"It's not a who, it's a what. Alfred Hitchcock uses them all the time. It means a deflection, a false lead. You're so sure it's important that you ignore everything around it."

"Are you telling me you think you've worked it out?"

"I think I'm maybe close, but I need to find Milligan to be sure."

"He's questioning Archie Love."

"Why's he doing that?"

"Remember three days ago, Jack? When Love was on our list because he wouldn't have been happy about his daughter seeing Carter?"

"Things have moved on." Laidlaw made to pass Lilley on his way to the door, but Lilley gripped his arm, just above the elbow. Laidlaw was surprised by how firm the grip was. Bob Lilley had muscle to him as well as heft. It would have served him well back in the days when he had trodden the beat as a constable.

"After I've spoken with Milligan, we'll go grab a drink," Laidlaw said. "I'll tell you my theory then. Deal?"

"And we'll set up a night for a meal round at ours?"

"You strike a hard bargain, Bob." Laidlaw looked to where his arm was still being held, waited while the pressure eased and his colleague released him. "Noon sharp in the Top Spot."

Lilley stared at Laidlaw's back as he left, even half thought of following him. But you didn't interfere with a force of nature, not if you knew what was good for you.

34

T hey weren't gathered in the meeting room of the Coronach Hotel this time, but in the drinking club where Laidlaw had found them playing cards. No card games today, just a table set with a single chair on which sat Cam Colvin. Every other chair in the room had been stacked, giving the clear hint that they were to stay standing. The barman, who had unlocked the door to let them in, had left by that same door. Spanner Thomson looked to Panda Paterson while Mickey Ballater and Dod Menzies exchanged questioning shrugs. Colvin had a mug of coffee in front of him. He took a slurp, placing it on the table afterwards as if repositioning a precious object in its display case.

"To say I'm disappointed would be the understatement of the year," he began, weighing each word by the ounce. "One of our best friends and closest colleagues is dumped behind a scabby pub and a week later we're no further forward. We've got to ask ourselves if that's because one of us isn't giving it a hundred per cent, which leads me to wonder why that might be the case."

Mickey Ballater's attention was on Spanner Thomson. He seemed taken aback when he realised everyone else was looking not at Spanner but at him. They were doing so in imitation of their boss. Ballater met Colvin's eyes.

"What's the game here?" he asked, brow furrowing.

"I should be asking you that, Mickey. Have you got a wee thing for the widow, eh? Fancy your chances there now Bobby's out of the picture?"

Ballater took a step towards Spanner Thomson, both hands curling into fists.

"Easy, Mickey," Colvin commanded.

"Fuck's sake, Cam. You're the one who fancies her—once that dawned on me, I backed all the way off. This is Spanner trying to turn the tables because you've got me watching him!"

"And how did he find out about that, Mickey? I'll tell you: you and your big fat trap!" Colvin rose slowly to his feet and came out from behind the table. Both his overcoat and suit jacket had been hung on pegs next to the bar. He was undoing his cufflinks and rolling up his shirtsleeves as he advanced on the group. "I need people around me I can trust. Neither of you seems to be fitting that particular bill."

Ballater's eyes were on Thomson again, his mouth as thin and firm a line as you would find along the bottom of a ledger. He seemed to make up his mind, throwing himself forward. He had given too much warning, however, and Thomson was already retreating a few steps, his hand sliding inside his coat. As the spanner emerged, wrapped in his fist, Ballater reached into his own pocket, pulling out a cut-throat razor, which opened with a flick of his wrist. Colvin snatched at Ballater's right arm and twisted it, pulling it up behind Ballater's back until the man's knees buckled, a silent cry escaping his throat. The razor clattered to the floor. The forefinger of Colvin's free hand was pointing in Thomson's direction.

"Back in your pocket, Spanner," he ordered.

"It's John Rhodes's pocket he's in!" Ballater called out.

Spanner Thomson ignored this, his attention focused on the man he'd known longer than anyone else in the city, longer even than his own wife.

"I need you to back me up here, Cam," he said. "I need to hear you say it in front of everyone."

"Say what, Spanner?"

"That you trust me."

"Doesn't seem the wisest of moves to trust anyone right now." Colvin glanced behind him. Paterson and Menzies had moved to the bar and armed themselves with bottles, ready to smash them, leaving jagged necks only. "Easy there, boys," he warned, scooping up the razor.

"Nobody touches my blade!" Ballater roared. "It was my dad's!"

"Do him while you can, Cam," Thomson spat. "Ask yourself who's more likely to have done away with Bobby. Who's hungry to sit in that chair next to you? And believe me, even that won't satisfy him for long."

"The pair of you need to shut the fuck up!" Colvin gave Ballater a shove, stepping away from his immediate orbit, his hand still clasped around the razor's scuffed ivory handle.

Panda Paterson was at Ballater's side, helping him to his feet. "Easy, Mickey, easy."

"I'm not the one that's tooled up, Panda."

Dod Menzies had put himself between Thomson and the others. He was holding both hands up as if in surrender, though one of them still held an empty mixer bottle.

"None of this is helping," he said.

"Cutting that bastard might, though," Thomson snarled. Menzies' free hand had begun reaching towards the raised spanner. The tool came down hard across his knuckles, causing him to gasp. He dropped the bottle, which shattered against the stone floor, and bent over, nursing the injury, muttering curses through gritted teeth.

"You're out of order, Spanner," Colvin said, his voice hoarse from the sudden adrenaline.

"As far as I can see, Cam, I'm the only one around here *not* out of order. And if that's the way it is, I suppose the only thing left to say is: fuck the lot of you. I don't want to hear from any of you after today, and if you come looking for me, you better be carrying heavy artillery."

"Spanner . . ."

Thomson looked at Cam Colvin. "Lot of history, Cam. And you've pissed all over it. I'm out." He turned and headed for the door.

"Good fucking riddance," Ballater called after him, rotating his shoulder as he checked it for damage.

"Spanner," Colvin repeated without any real force, eyes on the closing door. Ballater had retreated behind the bar, pouring himself a whisky. Menzies was flexing his fingers and wrist, wincing in pain.

"I need a check-up," he said.

"Surgery's open," Ballater informed him, setting a fresh glass on the bar next to the refilled ice bucket. Menzies plunged his hand into the ice. Paterson arrived alongside him, leaving Cam Colvin to stare at the door as if he could bring his old friend back by sheer force of will.

"You're better off without him," Ballater said. He had already regained a measure of composure, as if buoyed by Thomson's exit.

"He just needs a bit of time to think," Paterson speculated.

"That would be a first," Ballater said.

"You talk a lot of shite sometimes, Mickey, and you're transparent with it." Colvin was approaching the bar.

"Sorry, boss." Ballater poured another measure before holding out his hand, palm upwards. Colvin hesitated before passing him the razor, its blade folded again. He gave Ballater the hardest of stares, not relaxing until the razor was back in Ballater's pocket. Then he turned his attention to Menzies' hand.

"You okay?"

Menzies lifted his fist from the ice bucket. The knuckles were swelling and beginning to discolour. "I think something's broken." He gestured towards Ballater for a refill.

"When you've done that, Mickey," Colvin said, "I've got a job for you."

Ballater was suppressing a thin smile as he turned from the optics with Menzies' glass. "Anything you say, boss."

"That's good, because what I'm about to say is London."

Ballater's face was suddenly a creased question. "London?"

"Couple of business associates there. A deal's going down and I need eyes and ears in the room."

Ballater took a moment to process the information. Was this the back of the net or a sending-off? His face said he didn't have an answer.

"It's not for long," Colvin assured him.

"But with Spanner gone, you're already two men down."

"Plenty firepower in reserve, Mickey, don't you worry." Colvin glanced at his watch. "There's a train at noon—gives you time to go home and pack, if you start right now."

"Boss, I need to know—"

"No, you don't. I'll have someone meet you off the train. They'll take you to a hotel and I'll phone you." Colvin paused. "Always supposing that's okay with you?"

Paterson and Menzies were twitching, neither man able to work out if this meant the empty chair had been filled.

"You'll be back here before you know it," Colvin said. "But I need you to be on your way."

"If that's what you want, Cam."

"It is, Mickey."

Ballater considered for a further moment, then finished his drink. "I'll see you around, lads," he said to Paterson and Menzies, giving them a wave as he made for the door.

"Watch out for Spanner," Menzies called to him. "The man doesn't forget."

"Me neither, Dod, and I've yet to see a razor lose a fight . . ."

There was silence in the bar after he'd gone, as if a suspect device had been carted away. Colvin approached the optics and refilled each glass.

"Are you sure about this, Cam?" Panda Paterson asked.

"Time to regroup, lads. I want you to fetch me some fresh blood. Give me your best names and let's gather them around a table. I want them clever rather than stupid, able to give someone a fright but not Neanderthal. I appreciate it's a tall order . . ."

"I might know one or two," Paterson conceded.

"Me, too," Menzies added.

"By the end of the day, then, before the jungle drums start announcing recent departures."

"In the meantime, what do we do about Bobby?"

"Keep digging, keep asking. Somebody out there knows something."

"And John Rhodes? After what he did to Betty's taxis? We're due him some payback, no?"

"Are my ears burning?"

They all looked towards the doorway. A man with a heavily scarred face was holding it open while John Rhodes stood there silhouetted by the daylight behind. Both men walked in, the door rattling closed after them.

"This is unexpected, John," Colvin said.

Rhodes was studying Menzies' hand as it emerged from the ice bucket. "Which one did you punch, Spanner or Mickey?" He smiled for Cam Colvin's benefit. "I was in the car outside, weighing up my options. One of them was to have Gerry here hold shut the door while I torched the place."

"I had nothing to do with what happened at the Gay Laddie," Colvin stated.

"And I believe you." Rhodes nodded to himself. "Which is why I decided jaw-jaw was better than war-war. Now who do I have to French-kiss to get a drink here?" He had begun walking across broken glass towards the bar.

Colvin looked at the array of bottles below the row of optics. There were only two malts. He lifted the fuller one and released the cork stopper, pouring an inch into a glass and sliding it towards Rhodes.

"Have one yourself," Rhodes said. Then, turning towards Paterson and Menzies: "Not you two, though. You can fuck off outside. Gerry will keep you company. If you get bored, you can start comparing cocks. Got to warn you, though, his dad must have been more horse than man."

The two men looked to Colvin for their instructions. When he nodded, they made for the exit, the scarred man following them out. Colvin was refilling his own glass. He and Rhodes hoisted their drinks at the same time.

"Here's to business," Rhodes said, eyes fixed on Colvin's. He took his time as he nosed then sipped and savoured the malt. "The taxis had nothing to do with me," he said eventually.

"Who then?"

"I've got my suspicions."

"Matt Mason?"

Rhodes gave a look that could have meant anything. "I'm hoping to know for sure by the end of the day. I'll keep you posted."

"And I'm supposed to trust you?"

"That'll be up to you. But the way you're haemorrhaging men, any fight between us would be pretty one-sided."

"Don't count on that."

Rhodes allowed himself a smile. "You might like a scrap, but you're not the fighter you used to be—if you ever were."

"What do you mean by that?"

"The knife between your shoulders, the one thing everyone knows about you. Funny that when I went asking, no surgery or receptionist knew anything about it. Not that that matters—print the myth, as they say in the trade. But a myth lasts only so long."

"And you're immortal, are you?"

"Not at all. That's what separates us, Colvin—I know I'm only as good as the day I'm living." Rhodes tapped a meaty finger against the bar top. "Meaning this day right here." He watched Colvin try to process what he was saying. "Bit too philosophical for you? All right, change of tack—what's the score with Thomson and Ballater? Neither looked too thrilled when they stomped out."

"I know you talked to Spanner."

Rhodes offered a shrug. "I like to know what's going on. CID had him on their radar. I needed to find out how serious that was."

"And also whether he was ripe to switch sides." Colvin's eyes were on the door. He was wishing he hadn't given Ballater back the razor; doubted a broken bottle would be enough against Rhodes. The man had rested one buttock on a stool while Colvin remained on the serving side of the bar, fists bunched on top of a drip tray.

"You probably think I should have been to see you earlier," Rhodes said, "paying my respects and keen to convince you Bobby Carter's death had nothing to do with me?"

"Not really," Colvin answered. "Steering clear meant you looked confident, like you could afford to float above it all."

"I always knew you had your wits about you," Rhodes drawled. "Makes me wonder why you insist on surrounding yourself with the people you do."

"Same as you and Scarface, maybe. Neither of us likes competition."

"That may be a factor," Rhodes conceded before finishing his drink. "So what do we do now, you and me? Bit of naked wrestling on the floor? Pistols at dawn in Bellahouston Park?"

"I still need to know who killed Bobby."

"I'm not sure I can help you there."

"You positive about that?"

"The stuff that's been happening since, I'm going to get to the bottom of, but not Bobby Carter. If I take care of that bit of business, do we call a truce?"

"I'm not totally convinced I believe you about Bobby."

Rhodes peered into his drink and gave a sigh that would have passed muster on the stage of the Theatre Royal. "You know he was thinking of setting up on his own? Bobby, I mean. He wanted to discuss it with me."

"Why you rather than me?"

"Makes sense—if he could get the likes of me and Matt Mason on his side, it would make talking to you that bit easier."

Colvin shook his head. "I'll tell you what Bobby was doing—putting out feelers, because he had the notion someone was playing both sides."

"Are you sure about that? If you ask me, he'd seen too many Mafia flicks and thought the same shit would work in our Dear Green Place." Rhodes stared across the bar at Colvin. "I'm beginning to wonder if you really knew the guy at all. Maybe you just liked having him around because it meant you got to ogle his wife occasionally."

Colvin's eyes darkened and he squared his shoulders. Rhodes disarmed him with a smile as cold as a walk-in freezer. "You've been spotted at her house, Cam, that's all I'm saying. Next time you're there, ask to see Bobby's map of Glasgow. He didn't show it to me because I stood him up. But he did show it to Matt Mason. Apparently he was very proud of the way he'd only taken tiny bites out of Mason's territory and mine. You didn't fare quite as generously. That's why he needed Mason and me on board before he brought it to you. You weren't going to be happy about it, not happy at all. That's the kind of man you seem willing to raze this city to the ground for. Bear that in mind, eh? Whatever else Bobby Carter was, he was not your Robert fucking Duvall."

"You need to leave now before I do something I won't regret."

Rhodes slid from the stool, drawing himself to his full height.

"You come at me or mine, you better believe you'll regret it." His eyes were drawn to the glass strewn across the floor. "Bit of tidying-up to do, Colvin. Don't let me stop you fetching your dustpan."

"We cross paths again, you're a dead man."

"At least I'll be a dead man who never had to lie about getting knifed in the back."

Rhodes gave a wave of one leather-gloved hand as he made his exit. Colvin stood in silence for a moment before topping up his glass. His hand shook a little, but not much. He drained his drink, exhaled, then launched the emptied glass at the nearest wall.

35

L aidlaw knocked once on the door before entering and caught Ernie Milligan red-handed as he took possession of the football programme he'd just asked Archie Love to sign. He rolled it up and stuffed it into his pocket, trying to look unflustered.

"What do you want, Laidlaw?" he snapped.

"A word with you—if you've finished with the memorabilia." Laidlaw saw the swelling on Love's forehead. "If you need someone to corroborate that DI Milligan inflicted that injury, I'm your man."

"DC Laidlaw sometimes mistakes policing for an old episode of *Jokers Wild*," Milligan stated for Love's benefit.

"Seriously, though . . ." Laidlaw made show of examining the bruise. "Looks the sort of damage a hammer might do—a hammer or a spanner. Am I right?"

"I tripped in the dressing room," Love said.

"Of course you did." Laidlaw straightened up and followed Milligan out of the room. Milligan was scowling as he closed the door. He was about to say something, but Laidlaw got there first.

"Describe Bobby Carter's house to me."

"Didn't I see you there just yesterday?"

"You barred me from going inside, though, so humour me."

"Hallway, living room and kitchen, downstairs toilet, three bedrooms and a bathroom upstairs."

"Just the three bedrooms?"

"The boys share, though they're itching for their sister to move out so they can have a room each."

"Anything else?"

Milligan folded his arms while he considered. "Top-quality furniture, carpets are a bit loud for my taste. There's a decent-sized back garden plus a garage at the side."

"Car?"

"Vauxhall Victor estate, handy for a big family."

"Also handy for moving large objects," Laidlaw added thoughtfully.

"What the hell is all this?" Milligan sounded genuinely curious to know.

"You've not mentioned the redecorating."

"Okay."

"Whole house or just certain rooms?"

"The living room. Wall units moved into the downstairs hall. It was a bit of a bloody squeeze, to be honest."

"Carpets up?"

"Some, yes."

"Ladders and tins of paint?"

"Paint yes, ladders no. Satisfied?"

"I wouldn't go that far. You know the widow's ex is a painter and decorator?"

"It came up in the notes."

Laidlaw nodded to himself, then gestured towards the door. "Reckon you've got your man?"

"No."

"Just the autograph, then, eh?"

"He was some player in his day. You reckon Spanner Thomson did that damage?"

"Colvin's men are too gormless to do anything other than follow their noses, same as this inquiry's been doing."

Milligan's hackles rose perceptibly, but it was too late to do anything about it. Laidlaw had turned his back on him and was walking away. Milligan went after him.

"You need to tell me what you're doing. That's a direct order, DC Laidlaw."

"Kiss my hairy arse, DI Milligan."

"What's the house got to do with anything?"

"You're a detective. Given a few lifetimes, I'm sure even *you* can work it out."

A whisky apiece with a beer chaser, Bob Lilley given no say in the order. Then the same corner table as before, the one they'd sat at with Eck Adamson. The other drinkers consisted of two women surrounded by bags of purchases from a department store, and a couple of business suits at a separate table who looked as if the future of the world rested on their shoulders. One of the women was being taken to Paris the weekend after next, while the other had a new refrigerator on order.

"We've been looking in all the wrong places," Laidlaw said as Lilley settled next to him. It was as if his mind was half in the room and half elsewhere, like a medium tapping into the spirit world. "You might call it classic misdirection, but the murder itself was amateur hour. Think about it. The body was moved and then found. Why? A professional hit would have been cleaner and the body could have been buried under a motorway."

"The killer wanted it to be found."

"After a day or two, yes. But what was going on during that time?"

"Where are you going with this, Jack?"

"Who was it said early on—*cherchez la femme*? Most murders are domestic, Bob." Laidlaw met Lilley's gaze for the first time and held it. "Bobby enjoyed the company of other women, but at home he ruled with an iron fist. Neighbour across the way heard regular arguments. Monica's ex-husband wasn't allowed over the threshold. It wasn't so much a family in that house as a hostage situation. Not that we focused on any of that; we were too busy making the facts suit our pre-conceived ideas. Gangsters get hit by other gangsters, end of story. And to be fair to us, there was no end of suspects to keep us busy and stop us seeing what was in front of our faces." He paused. "In fact I blame Milligan for that one hundred per cent. If he'd allowed a proper detective to enter that house, they'd maybe have twigged sooner, but he kept that wee treat to himself. Stupid of us to let him do that."

"Twigged what, though?"

"The whole house was redecorated a couple of months back, Bob."

"I'm not sure what you're getting at."

"This murder was messy and spontaneous and personal. It then took time to work out what had to happen next. Take the body to John Rhodes's part of town and plant it there; get rid of the knife close to where one of Cam Colvin's team lives. Planned by someone who knew a bit about both camps. Spanner's address would be known to anyone near the top of the Colvin hierarchy. The Parlour was where Bobby Carter was due to meet John Rhodes, except Rhodes bailed. Carter would have been fuming about that, maybe said something about it to someone close to him."

Lilley was shaking his head as if to refuse the invitation Laidlaw was offering him. "I was beginning to enjoy working with you, Jack—if that's what you can call what we've been doing. But now I'm not so sure."

"I don't like it either, Bob, but the truth's not about likes and dislikes, it just *is*. And if you liking me is dependent on me lying to you or giving you soft options, forget it."

"You saw the family, though—the photos in the paper, the TV pictures. They were devastated."

"Of course they were." Laidlaw paused. "They'd just murdered the head of the household."

Lilley snorted in disbelief. "You're saying all of them did it, based solely on someone telling you the place had been redecorated recently?"

"Good people do bad things all the time, Bob. Especially when they feel trapped or lied to and let down over and over again. Our job, yours and mine, is to uphold the law, especially when turning a blind eye means other people getting hurt. What we had here was a classic case of the giant's fingers."

"You've lost me again."

"It's something John Updike said—details are like the giant's fingers. No matter how big and complex something is, it all comes down to smaller details." Laidlaw saw the blank look on his partner's face. "Okay then, how about W. H. Auden? His poem 'Musée des Beaux Arts.' Friend of mine at school, Tom Docherty, he was a big fan. 'About suffering they were never wrong, the Old Masters.' Auden is looking at Brueghel's painting *The Fall of Icarus*. There's this calamity happening—Icarus falling to his death—but nobody in the painting is paying any attention to it, too distracted by their everyday concerns."

"Right."

"You're a proper philistine, aren't you?"

"Plain talk and plain bread are my staples, if that's what you mean."

"So what do you say?"

"To what?"

"To coming with me."

"Bearsden, you mean?"

"Where else?"

"You don't think you should maybe clear it with Milligan first?"

"No."

"Or put together a case that's more than an amalgamation of guesswork and lines from poems I've never heard of?"

Laidlaw offered a shrug and said nothing.

"You're going anyway, aren't you?" Lilley looked resigned to the fact.

"I'm going anyway," Laidlaw agreed.

36

When they parked outside the house in Bearsden, Laidlaw gave a wave to Mrs. Jamieson, who was peering, sentinel-like, from a gap in her net curtains. They were halfway up the path to the Carter house when its door opened, Cam Colvin paying them no heed as he stomped towards his own car. The two detectives paused to watch him.

"Was that a street map he was holding?" Lilley enquired.

"You'd think by now he'd know his way around the city," Laidlaw agreed, tapping at the open door and stepping into the hallway. He could smell fresh paint. Whatever clutter had been in the hall, however, was no longer there. From what he could see, only the one wall here had actually had a fresh coat—the one running along the side of the staircase. He indicated as much to Bob Lilley before entering the living room. All three children—Stella, Peter and Chris—were seated there, books and comics on their laps. Their mother stood at the entrance to the kitchen. She looked jittery, Cam Colvin no doubt to blame.

"Caught you at a bad time?" Laidlaw asked.

"Who the hell are you?"

It was Stella who answered her mother. "He's the policeman I told you about."

Laidlaw had walked towards the shelving unit. It was filled with paperbacks, a mix of recent bestsellers and weightier non-fiction collections.

"I always think you can tell a lot about someone from their bookcases," he said. "This one, for example, was in the hall a few days back."

"So?"

"You told Ernie Milligan it was because you were getting the place painted." Laidlaw made show of studying his surroundings. Monica Carter had settled herself on the arm of the chair her daughter sat on. "But this room's not been touched at all, Mrs. Carter."

"Started with the downstairs hall."

Laidlaw began to shake his head. "You had the whole house redecorated a couple of months back." The teenagers had given up any pretence of reading and their eyes were on him. "No smell of fresh paint in here, just in the hall. Yet for some reason you moved the bookcase. It's a solid bit of wood, too. No cheap rubbish for you. I'd guess it would take at least a couple of people to shift it. Question is: why move it at all?"

"You tell me." Monica Carter's look was all challenge, as if squaring up for a bar brawl.

Bob Lilley had taken a route around the perimeter of the room and was checking that there were no surprises in the kitchen. He shook his head in confirmation.

"You really want me to do that, Mrs. Carter?" Laidlaw said. "Very well then—either you didn't have time at first to do the painting, or you managed only the one coat and that wasn't enough. The shelves were to cover the stains until you could do a better job." He paused. "By stains, I mean bloodstains, of course; your husband's bloodstains."

Suddenly the room was a tumult of noise as Monica Carter and her children began to protest. Laidlaw allowed it for a few seconds, then held up a hand. "I need everybody to shut the fuck up!" he yelled.

The room froze, turning the family into sudden statues.

"You should engage a lawyer," Laidlaw went on, his tone neutral. "I can suggest a good one if you're stuck."

"He hit her," Stella was saying. "Even stubbed out a cigarette on her wrist."

"He was a bastard," her brother Chris added. He was the youngest, and resembled both his father and older brother, while Stella was more like her mother. "A bastard to all of us."

Laidlaw nodded slowly and solemnly. He had planted his feet in front of fourteen-year old Peter, who was staring into space as if trying to make up his mind about something momentous.

"How about you, son?" he asked.

It was as if a switch had been flipped. Peter leaped to his feet, drawing a flick knife from his pocket, its tip aimed at Laidlaw. Laidlaw feinted to one side and as the blade approached managed to wrap his fist around the boy's bony wrist, twisting until the knife fell to the floor. He shoved Peter back onto the sofa and crouched to pick up the weapon. The room had grown noisy again, and Monica Carter dashed forward to hug her son. She squeezed in next to him and he didn't shrug her off. All the same, his eyes were trained on Laidlaw, and there was plenty of fire still in them.

"Looks like we've found our killer," Bob Lilley commented.

"It wasn't Peter, it was me," Stella argued, rising to her feet.

Laidlaw waved her back down. "This isn't *Spartacus*, Stella. Having said which, I've seen worse defence strategies than everybody blaming each other. Jury might have a tough job deciding between you all, based on the evidence. You could end up with 'not proven.'" He paused again, his eyes on Monica. "But you know what the problem with that is, don't you, Mrs. Carter?"

"Cam Colvin," she answered quietly.

"Colvin still needs to extract justice. If nobody goes away, you can expect a knock on the door one night. It doesn't particularly matter to me which one of you wielded the knife—maybe you all took turns. But once the deed was done, you definitely acted in concert, didn't you? Did the body go into the garage first of all? If so, we'll find blood there. Same goes with the fresh paint—it might hide, but it never erases. Back of your estate car? Same thing." Laidlaw could see that his words were getting through to the widow. "What did Colvin want, by the way?"

"He grabbed a map from the shelves." It was Stella who had spoken.

"Don't know why," her mother added. Then, having come to a decision: "It was me, just me and me alone." She looked at each of her children in turn. "I need you to let me do this, do you hear? I killed him and none of you knew anything about it." She turned her attention back to Laidlaw. "Is that acceptable?"

"It's not me you have to convince."

"So do I hand myself in or what?"

"We can give you an hour's grace, long enough to sort things out here. If you're not at Central Division soon afterwards, you can expect us to be back with blue lights flashing and bells ringing."

"Thank you," she said.

Stella had crossed to the sofa and placed herself next to her mother, so that all four sat in the closest possible proximity, like creatures huddled together for warmth, wary of the coming winter.

"The lawyer you want is Bryce Mundell," Laidlaw said, before gesturing towards Lilley and making his exit.

In the hall, Lilley asked in an undertone if Laidlaw was sure the family wouldn't make a run for it. Laidlaw shook his head.

"They've been waiting for us," he said. "Patiently, all this time. We're what they know needs to happen."

They had just reached the car when another drew up. Ernie Milligan stepped out, his anger focused on Laidlaw.

"What did I tell you?" he said.

"Never mind that—here's what *I'm* telling *you*. We're off to make a report to the Commander. That report will detail who murdered Bobby Carter and what happened in the aftermath. It will also flag up that if a *real* detective rather than a jobsworth with a hard-on had been allowed into that house earlier, this would have been done and dusted and a lot of grief might have been spared. So instead of whispering any further sweet nothings to the widow, I suggest you follow us in your car. Trust me, you don't want to miss out."

Laidlaw didn't wait to hear what Milligan had to say by way of reply. He climbed into the passenger seat while Lilley started the engine. Milligan went from tapping on the window to pulling at the door handle, but Laidlaw had pushed down the lock with one hand while turning the other into a pistol, which he pointed at the road ahead, indicating that Lilley shouldn't hang around.

As they moved off, they watched Milligan in the rearview mirror as he scrambled to get back into his own car.

"Are you really going to land him in it?" Lilley asked.

"Every chance I get, Bob," Laidlaw answered, leaning back and closing his eyes.

37

S eated behind his desk, Robert Frederick stared at the two detectives. Bob Lilley had taken a seat, on which he writhed and twisted as if racked by doubt. Jack Laidlaw, conversely, stood legs apart, arms by his sides, like an imposing statue erected in honour of some self-confident warrior prince.

Seeing the sceptical look on the Commander's face, Lilley felt obliged to break the silence.

"She did confess, sir."

"According to Jack here, they *all* did, more or less."

"If we can muster a forensic team to look at the paintwork . . ."

"First call I need to make is to the fiscal. It's them that'll need convincing."

"Them and you both by the sound of it," Laidlaw announced under his breath.

The Commander glowered at him. "There are procedures, Jack, and a reason for those procedures. Why didn't you arrest them at the house if you're so sure your theory holds water?"

"Due respect, sir, my theory could float the *Ark Royal*."

"Nobody likes a smartarse."

"Nobody likes Milligan either, yet he keeps rising through the ranks, almost as if a few secret handshakes beats possession of a brain."

Colour suffused the Commander's cheeks.

"What Jack means is—"

"Bob, you'd do well to keep your gob shut," Frederick shot

back. "A DS and a DC don't get to barge into someone's house and accuse them of murder. With their kids sitting right there next to them? Defence would have a field day in court. Any suspicions should have gone to Ernie Milligan and from him to the fiscal. Mrs. Carter has now been forewarned, which means if she's got any sense she'll be engaging a lawyer and maybe even conferring with her offspring so they get their version of events straight. What happens if we go back there and she denies everything?"

"We check the car and the garage," Laidlaw intoned, "see if there's maybe a knife missing from the kitchen drawer."

"When I want your advice, I'll request it in writing."

"It's Ernie Milligan you should be talking to. He's the one who could have had this done and dusted if he possessed even half an ounce of savvy."

"Instead of which," Bob Lilley added, "we've had days of escalation, two gangs ready to lay waste to each other—"

"I get that, Bob," the Commander broke in. "But does your pal here get that his methods might have jeopardised any prosecution?"

"I did what needed doing," Laidlaw said, meeting the Commander's gaze.

Robert Frederick leaned back in his chair, shaking his head slowly, looking suddenly weary. There was a knock at the door. Without waiting to be asked, a head appeared. It was Frederick's secretary.

"Sorry, sir," she said.

"Can't it wait, Sally?"

"I'm not sure it can, sir. Woman at the front desk by the name of Carter. Says she's here to make a confession. Thing is, it's DC Laidlaw she's asking to see. Says she'll talk to him and him alone . . ."

38

At the Top Spot, drinks were on the Commander. There was no sign of the women shoppers or the self-important suits. A game of darts had been convened, two competing teams assembled, Laidlaw and Lilley content to prop up the bar while they watched. The room was wreathed in smoke. Lilley knew he would pay for it when he got home. Margaret would insist he put everything in the laundry and head to the shower, the shower itself a rubber hose pushed onto the two taps in the bath. The hose had never fitted properly and one side or the other would invariably become dislodged, so that you ended up with scalding or freezing water, usually timed to coincide with a head covered in soap suds.

"Can we appear for the defence, do you think?" Laidlaw was asking, not for the first time. His eyes were slightly glazed as he attempted to deal with the constant stream of drinks placed in front of him. "I mean, are there precedents?"

"Will Colvin settle for the result, that's what I'm wondering?"

"He better, or else he'll have me to deal with, and now that we've done away with hanging, I'm more sanguine about the consequences of doing him in."

"Would your philosophers say the same thing?"

"I'd happily argue my case in front of them." Laidlaw stared at the bottom of his emptied glass. "She's about to serve a second sentence, Bob, the first being her marriage. She played that role as best she could until she had to disrupt the performance. Or maybe she was a skater, the ice breaking under her, the depths below dark as sin. Didn't matter how well she skated, how balletically and confidently she moved, the darkness was there waiting for her. Whatever else happens, the dark remains."

"Lucky for us that it does, or we'd be down the dole office."

Laidlaw gave a twitch of the mouth and eased himself away from the bar, walking with the stiff uprightness of the lightly inebriated towards the toilets. The Commander approached Lilley, clapping him on the shoulder.

"Your boy did all right in the end, almost despite himself," he said.

"He defused your city, if that's what you mean."

"If he doesn't manage to detonate himself in the near future, he might be in line for a swift promotion."

"That's bound to please DI Milligan." Lilley looked around the bar. "Where is he anyway?"

"Licking his wounds elsewhere. Though if you ask him, he'll say he's swotting up on the case, preparatory to interviewing the family members."

"I hear the mother has engaged the services of Bryce Mundell."

The Commander nodded. "Though with her confession, all he's going to be doing is scratching around for mitigating circumstances."

"Plenty of those, I would think."

"So what do you reckon to Jack Laidlaw, Bob? Truthfully, I mean, just between the two of us."

Lilley didn't have to think about it. "He's the business."

"Meaning?"

"He's a one-off in a world of mass production. He's not a copper who happens to be a man. He's a man who happens to be a copper, and he carries that weight with him everywhere he goes." His words were surprising him while he spoke them aloud. He hadn't realised until this moment how strongly he agreed with them. "Mind you," he felt it necessary to qualify, "he can be a pain in the bahookie, too, but it's a price worth paying."

The words seemed to percolate, the Commander nodding slowly afterwards. "Noted," he said, pretending to watch the darts game. "Not exactly a team player, though."

"I wouldn't say darts is his forte."

There was a cheer and a victorious raising of arms as one team checked out. Lilley and his boss watched as the scores were immediately wiped from the chalkboard with a cloth. Laidlaw was checking his fly as he returned to the bar.

"Good work, Jack," the Commander said, handing him a fresh tumbler of Antiquary.

"It's not difficult—doesn't everyone check afterwards that they've zipped up?"

"That's not what I was talking about."

"I know," Laidlaw said, clinking his glass against the Commander's before taking another large swallow.

39

The blood had dried to a crust on Malky Chisholm's face. The damage was superficial: just a couple of blows to the nose. Those punches could hurt, though. They could crush cartilage and send tears streaming from your eyes. One of Chisholm's teeth had been loosened, too. He both knew and didn't know where he was. It was a lock-up garage. That much had been evident from the moment the hessian sack had been removed from his head. And the fact that John Rhodes was pacing the floor in front of him meant it was probably in the Calton somewhere. Could be any one of a dozen streets, anonymous as well as private. Chisholm had heard no traffic going past, no snatches of conversation between pedestrians from beyond the breeze-block walls. This was one of those places where Rhodes could conduct his business without fear of interruption or consequence.

"I don't know why I didn't figure it out sooner," Rhodes was saying. He was dressed in a zipped jacket, roomy denims and cheap canvas shoes. Chisholm didn't need to be told what the outfit meant. All of it was disposable, and it would be disposed of later that night. The man with the scarred face was standing guard by the door to the outside world. Fumes lingered in the air, hinting that a vehicle of some kind had been moved out just prior to Chisholm's enforced arrival. He'd been grabbed on the street, a hood pulled over his head before he was thrown into the back of a van. It had all been very professional. Chisholm liked to think that his crew would be as slick a machine in the circumstances, though he doubted it. John Rhodes, he was beginning to realise, was the real deal, and, moreover, a man you crossed at your peril, that peril being imminent extinction.

"I mean," Rhodes went on, "it was a matter of elimination. Did it make sense for it to be Cam Colvin? Of course it did. It made too much sense, that was the problem. But then when the taxis got hit, well, I knew I'd not ordered that, so who had? And did that mean someone was attacking both of us in the hope of the conflict escalating?" He stopped and bent a little, the better to be at eye level with his prisoner. Chisholm was seated on a wooden chair of the type more commonly found at a school desk, his hands tied behind him, ankles bound to the chair legs with twine. The knots were tight, producing pins and needles in his feet. There was electrical tape across his mouth, meaning he had to breathe through his bloodied nostrils.

"You see what I'm saying?" Rhodes went on. "That meant my next port of call was Matt Mason, who denied having anything to do with it. He could have been lying, of course. You never know with a bastard like him. But he sounded genuine enough, and he's had other things on his mind, with the hospital and everything."

He broke off, straightening up and beginning to pace again, like some caged predator. It was a narrow space. Four strides and he was at the tool-strewn workbench. When he turned, a few further paces took him to the wall opposite, where a selection of electrical leads hung from rusted nails.

"Then," he continued, "I started thinking about you. I started thinking about you long and hard. A junior with his eyes on the boardroom. Whose boardroom, though? I'm not sure that even matters. But Bobby Carter's death was like you'd been picked for *The Golden Shot*. The bolt was already loaded. You just had to aim it at the thread connecting me and Cam Colvin."

Yes, Chisholm could have told him, and it was Jack Laidlaw

who planted the seed that day in the interview room. Attack both fiefdoms, ramp up the chaos, watch them tear one another apart. As all hell breaks loose on the streets, the Cumbie sits there waiting to come crawling out once the dust settles on the battlefield. It had seemed almost too easy, and it had almost worked.

Almost.

The pacing had stopped again. Rhodes stood less than a yard from the seated figure and seemed to study him before walking behind Chisholm and placing his hands firmly on the younger man's shoulders. With infinite slowness, the chair was tipped back until Chisholm could do nothing but stare at the face poised above him. Rhodes's tone when speaking had been relaxed, almost laconic, but his look now was one of pure and unbridled malevolence.

"So do I skin you myself or hand you over to Cam Colvin?" he asked, teeth bared.

Behind the gag, Chisholm was trying to speak. Rhodes considered for a moment, then ripped the tape off, causing the young man to screw shut his eyes in momentary pain.

"Your decision," he managed eventually, hoping he sounded less panicked than he felt. He was having to work hard at stopping his bladder and bowels from emptying. "But there's a third option, too."

"Oh aye?"

"I could be an asset to you, a real asset. I bring a whole squad with me who'll do whatever they're told."

"Whack guys on the street? Firebomb a pub? Batter the windscreens out of a fleet of taxis?" Rhodes took a moment to consider this. "And you'd be willing to work for me, follow my orders?"

"Seems to me it beats the alternatives. Look, whether or not I had anything to do with the Gay Laddie and the beatings and the damage to the cabs, I can be useful to—"

Rhodes had heard enough. The tape was stuck back over Malky Chisholm's mouth, Rhodes squeezing it hard beneath the heel of his hand to ensure it was secure. The chair was dropped back onto all four legs again. Chisholm watched as Rhodes approached the door where the scarred man stood. The two exchanged a few muttered words. Then the scarred man nodded, his eyes on Chisholm, as John Rhodes opened the door and stepped out briskly into the sodium night. The scarred man walked towards the workbench and ran his fingers over some of the tools lying there.

He seemed to be looking for something in particular. Eventually he found it. It was wrapped in an oily-looking piece of muslin cloth. Slowly and surely he began to peel the layers of cloth away while Malky Chisholm watched, the blood pounding in his ears. He felt like he was falling with infinite slowness from a very great height, though in the full and certain knowledge that the fall itself was not going to be the death of him.

The revealed revolver, however, was another story entirely.

T hat night, Laidlaw lay in his bed at the Burleigh Hotel, Jan asleep in his wakeful arms. With the case closed, he knew he could be at home, but he needed one more night on this life raft. The Commander had hinted at a promotion, but Laidlaw couldn't help thinking a leper's bell might prove more appropriate. He turned his thoughts to Monica Carter. She would shift all the weight to her own broad shoulders. Her children would visit her in prison. He realised he would like to visit her, too, but he knew he never would. Such a visit might salvage something for him but would be poison to her, once the other inmates worked out what he was. He had known good people go bad before, had visited his fair share of toxic relationships, marriages seemingly fine on the outside but rotting from the core. Abusive partners, mental and physical cruelty, children little more than cannon fodder, themselves growing up damaged and ready to repeat the mistakes of their parents, knowing no other way of living and being. He wondered about Stella and Peter and Chris. What did the future hold for them? His mind was on Peter especially, with his ready knife and his eyes ablaze. Had he just got away with murder? If so, where might that eventually lead?

He tried not to think of his own wife and children. That way led to a deeper, darker ocean of hurt. Instead, he felt his arms envelop Jan. I'm clinging on for dear life, he thought to himself. Please let me see the morning . . .

ABOUT THE AUTHORS

William McIlvanney is widely credited with being the founder of the Tartan Noir movement that includes authors such as Denise Mina, Ian Rankin, and Val McDermid, all of whom cite him as an influence and inspiration. McIlvanney's Laidlaw trilogy "changed the face of Scottish fiction" (*The Times of London*). His novel *Docherty* won the Whitbread Award for Fiction, and both *Laidlaw* and *The Papers of Tony Veitch* won CWA Silver Dagger Awards. *Strange Loyalties* won the *Glasgow Herald*'s People's Prize. McIlvanney passed away in December 2015.

New York Times best-selling and Edgar Award-winning author Ian Rankin was born in the Kingdom of Fife. His first John Rebus novel, *Knots and Crosses*, was published in 1987. The Rebus series is now translated into twenty-two languages and the books are bestsellers on several continents. Rankin has received an OBE for services to literature. In addition to the Edgar Award, Rankin is also recipient of a Gold Dagger for Fiction and the Chandler-Fulbright Award. He lives in Edinburgh, Scotland, with his wife and their two sons.